INQUESTOR TALES

Despatches from the High Inquest • Number One • July, 2018
Diplodocus Press • Bangkok • Los Angeles

Contents

© 2018 by Somtow Sucharitkul. All rights to material not by Somtow Sucharitkul are the
property of their creators.
ISBN: 978-1940999241

Diplodocus Press
Bangkok • Los Angeles
www.diplodocuspress.com

Message from the High Inquest

Is anybody there?

In 1985, the last Inquestor novel was published by Bantam. It was, in some ways, an ill-fated series. My first professional sale, *The Thirteenth Utopia*, published in the April 1979 issue of *Analog*, had introduced the world of the High Inquestors, and the story made quite a splash, missing a Hugo nomination by only two votes, I'm told; the series itself came into being in spurts, a short story here, a novelette there, mostly in the pages of *Asimov's Science Fiction Magazine*, thanks to the energy and encouragement of George Scithers.

In 1982 came *Light on the Sound*, a full length novel in this universe, followed swiftly by its sequel, *The Throne of Madness*. I was young. The stories were getting a lot of attention. People I admired greatly were praising them: Orson Scott Card, Theodore Sturgeon, Robert Bloch ... and there were those reviews: the Washington *Post*, *Publishers Weekly*, the L.A. *Times*. In 1983, I was a rising star of science fiction, but a few years later, everything changed. It looked as if this trilogy was going to be the first step in a slew of trilogies and I'd have a series as popular as any of the others at the time to which it was being compared ... but it was not to be.

First, my publisher, *Timescape*, went through a bit of a reorganization and basically downsized, leaving the third volume of my trilogy in limbo. In other words, there were two volumes of a trilogy in print, but they were sort of cutting off the *Timescape* brand and therefore not going to publish the third book.

Then, the publisher who took me up next, Bantam, wanted to do the whole trilogy, but since the first two books had gone out of print and were from a different publisher, they wanted a new approach, so I suggested taking all the Inquestor novelettes and short stories that were in print, and weaving them together with a framing story that could be a different way of introducing the final volume of the trilogy. And so *Utopia Hunters* came about.

Utopia Hunters introduced characters from different timelines who had never appeared in the first two volumes of the trilogy, and so *The Darkling Wind* became *both* the third volume of a trilogy with the first two books from *Timescape,* and the second volume of a two-book series beginning with *Utopia Hunters* and carrying on the story of the characters who first appeared there as well. *The Darkling Wind* was therefore a *fat* book, because it was the third volume of one series *and* the second volume of another, all merged together.

These four books are, as far as I know, the *only* example of a *five-book trilogy in four volumes.* It was a level of mathematical complexity beyond my publishers, who as soon as they reprinted the first two books in the series, put the second two out of print.

During their heyday as it were — at no time was the entire series ever all available at the same time — and never from the same publisher.

These decisions made by executives in New York were based on big picture issues — the lives and deaths of entire lines of books, not the survival of a single midlist author. But effectively, the decisions reduced the books to a special-interest commodity, sought after only by true believers. And I rather despaired of science fiction and as my readers know, I drifted towards other fields ... and in the early 21st century, I found myself doing more and more music (my first profession) so that my writing career of 50 plus novels and books seemed more and more like a side trip on the convoluted journey of my artistic career.

So ... time goes by. Three decades in fact. Once in a while, I get letters. They are of the "Whatever happened to..." variety mostly. I discover that there's a small number of people with battered, wornout copies of these books. In the words of one of them, "I've lent them out so many times that they've fallen apart ... I wish I could get new copies."

I had all the rights back by then, so a couple of years ago I entered the brave new world of print on demand, turned myself into a my own publishing company, and quietly slipped everything I ever wrote back into print. For the first time, all four the books were available at the same time, and all from the same publisher. What's more, there was no middle man between author and reader. I was like a bard singing for my supper at the dinner table of a mediaeval lord. The history of publishing had cycled back to its beginnings.

It didn't matter than only one or two copies sold each month; it was like free money. Those people trying to replace their wornout copies were keeping the series alive.

At some point, these same people started asking for more.

There is a lot more to say in this world. I realized that after it lay to one side for three decades. For each doorway I opened, I left a dozen more still sealed.

My first thought was to get back into the series via some "juveniles" as they used be called, with young protagonists — shorter novels like Anne McCaffrey's *Harper Hall* books which develop alongside the heftier Pern books. This is why I started looking at the character of Sajit, who we first meet in the short story *The Rainbow King* which is reprinted in this first issue of *Inquestor Tales*. My first thought was to write a simple, brief story of Sajit's childhood — a childhood talked about briefly in the existing canon — a dirt poor street kid, neglected, abused, clinging to music and finally pulled into the Inquestor world through an accidental encounter with the young Inquestor Elloran.

But as I thought about telling his story, which would have been an easy story to tell, because nothing could be simpler for me than to weave the same tapestry I've woven before to the same pattern; the pleasure city of Alykh in a way is sort of a mega-Bangkok, so all I'd have to do is sit where I am and close my eyes and start imagining just a little bit. But then a different character began speaking to me, and I had to find a way of reconciling the two, somehow. So, without spoiling it for you, I'll just say that the pathway led in a more convoluted direction than I originally thought it would.

However, in this first installment out of perhaps four to six, there's not much complication yet. You'll have to wait for the second installment, *The Woman Cloaked in Shadow,* to see how complication begins to set in.

So what you hold in your hands is something retrogressively and militantly fannish: it is essentially a *personalzine*. It's an bit of an exercise in narcissism. It also reveals that despite the fact that I've had many requests to return to the Inquestor universe — indeed, to return to science fiction itself, because my absconding into the horror world was seen by some as a betrayal — in some ways I still see myself as a young and geekish person awed by the ideas of science fiction's Golden Age. I never left that world.

We've come a ways since those mimeographed stapled things that came in the mail, but I have boxes of them somewhere. Personalzines were the printed ancestors of blogs, I suppose. But each issue consisted almost entirely of the lunatic ravings of a single person. The miracle of print on demand now makes it possible to produce such a product with the veneer of professionality, a color cover, in actual pulp size though on nicer paper.

So, each issue of *Inquestor Tales* will contain, for those who have been asking for three decades, a hefty installment of a new Inquestor novel, until such time as the book is done. It'll be filled out with an Inquestor story from the 1980s in original form (i.e. unchanged since it appeared then, not the form in which they were eventually subsumed into the printed books. From time to time, my friends will contributed a piece here and there. I'll also have some articles about Inquestral linguistics, and other background material from my age-old notes which no one has ever seen. When I run out of Inquestor short stories from the past, I suppose I will have to produce new ones. As befits a personalzine, I don't doubt that I shall also have the odd rant, or tidbits about my life, or rare reprints that don't have anything to do with Inquestors.

There will also be a lettercolumn. There's a lettercolumn in this very first issue, by the way, even though people haven't read the new book yet. At least, there's some commentary. "Actual" letters will come soon and I hope you'll write them.

I envisage this as being bimonthly or quarterly, but reserve the right to be completely irregular as befits a true personalzine.

Mikey Jiraros

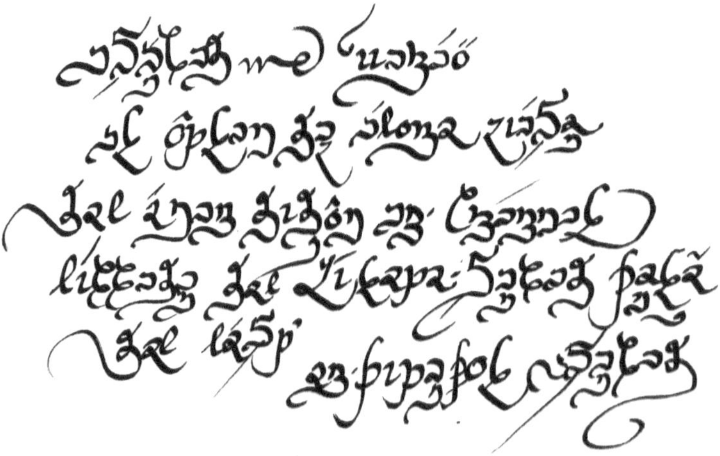

CHRONICLES OF THE HIGH INQUEST
The Homeworld of the Heart

by S.P. Somtow

Book One
THE SINGING MOONS

evéndek evéndek hyeméo
et órten kes éluma sieváh
kal ánem kikrón em-zmémnet
líddeken kal chítara 'vendek shãtráh
kal lavr' ã-shirénzhut evéndek

Always, always, I come home
to a place that the spirit knows
though the mind has long forgotten;
to a song that the heart still sings
though the lips have been silenced forever.

— from the Songs of Sajit

Prologue
Sajittang

... and there was also a village named Sajittang ...

•••

... far from the great central worlds of the Dispersal ... at the opposite end of the galaxy from Uran s'Varek, the sphere of the Inquestors that surrounds the black hole at the galaxy's heart, where the stars are packed so thick that their scattered light, through thousands of klomets of atmosphere, blends and blurs to a seamless radiance ... whose thinkhive contains the thoughts of a billion billion souls ...

... far from Gallendys with its pyramidal twin cities stacked one upon the other like cones of pinwheel fire, where the windbringers fly blindly and sing music of searing light ...

... far from Shtoma, where they dance on the face of the sun ...

... far from Aëroësh, where the dust is alive and the living turn to dust ...

... far from Periput, from Bellares, from Billoras, from Bellbaros, from Anthalafré and Ugoradé, from the chimes of Chembrith, from the feasting fields of Fiünn and the forever forests of Fáraklanth ...

Sajittang was the only village on this world; a single pair of displacement plates linked it with a starport, to which few pilgrims came. When they came, they would come to the shrine in Sajittang, where an old whisperlyre lay on a plinth beneath a protective forceshield.

This shrine, this starport, should not even exist, for the world has *fallen beyond*. But pilgrims did come, from time to time, and they would visit the whisperlyre, guarded by orphaned srinjids, and they would meditate a while, or kiss the barrier of force as if to get closer to the whisperlyre, or try to write a poem as they sat in the village square.

But one day, there came a visitor more important than most...

***

Varezhdur, palace of dreams, hung in the night sky like a spindle trailing threads of gold, eclipsing the moons themselves. And from the palace a floater delicately descended.

An old man flanked by srinjids watched. The old man had waited all his life for this moment to come. He knew that one day a floater would come, and who would be riding it. What surprised him was that the man was alone. It was a figure he dared not look at closely; to gaze such a one directly in the eyes had been known to bring immediate execution. But he was alone. There was not even a quartet of child-soldiers guarding the four corners of the railings, the minimum escort for one of such power.

The floater moved in a completely straight line, though there was a wind, whispering as it scattered dead leaves over the flag-stones.

"Now," said the old man to the srinjids, "begin your song."

Childlike, one srinjid spoke and another answered. The two voices harmonized almost without intent. From a hut behind the shrine, another voice came, then another, speaking of inconsequential things, yet each inconsequently snippet of speech was an ornament, a trill, a heterophonous melisma woven into an overarching music.

The srinjid's song was of necessity complete; their city on Uran s'Varek long destroyed, but a handful of refugees had been rescued. Here, in Sajittang, they thrived, but their song was not a perfect melding of a million voices; it was the ghost of a song, a snatch here, an echo there; it was a memory of what was once beautiful, not the beautiful thing itself. Yet it had its own melancholy beauty, even in its imperfection.

The floater touched the flagstones of the square, old stucco stained with age, veined with a purple moss from which one could distill a *zul*-like liquor. The old man had not seen any pilgrims for a long time, years; this was no ordinary pilgrim. The floater's skin dissolved. The old man prostrated himself. It was a moment he had rehearsed for all his life, yet now that it had come, there was an emptiness to it; the time when such gestures had meaning was long past.

Through unkempt white strands of his own hair, the old man saw the shadow of a shimmercloak. The coruscating pink against deep blue. The cloak that was a living thing, gliding, flowing, intertwining flesh. And feet; immaculately manicured, bare, but painted with protective shieldskin; this Inquestor was old, too, but for an Inquestor, to be old is different different.

"Hokh'Ton," the old man mumbled, then waited to be spoken to.

"What are you called?" Strangely high-pitched, a child's voice, almost, though the flesh was withered.

"I am Tash Toléon," he replied, "of the Clan of Rememberers. I guard the tomb of Shen Sajit, the voice of the cosmos."

"Stand, Tolé," said the Inquestor. "My feet do not have ears, and I'm too old to bend down to your level."

Toléon motioned for one of the srinjids to bring a stool. Another fetched some of the juice of the moss. "Forgive me," Tash Toléon said. "Seeing you in the flesh —"

"So you know my name," the Inquestor said.

"Of course. You are hokh'Ton Ton Elloran n'Taanyel Tath, Lord of Varezhdur."

"What else do you know?"

"That you knew Shen Sajit when you were children. That you showed him favor beyond all measure. It was even said that he was your lover."

And Ton Elloran smiled a little at that, saying only, "Love has a million shapes."

For a while Elloran listened to the singing of the srinjids. "I didn't know the remnants of that city were here," he said. "It is ... painful to hear. You never heard their singing city, of course."

"No, hokh'Ton."

"It's like hearing a ghost."

"Everything on this world is a ghost," said Toléon. "Including myself, for I exist only to be your rememberer."

He nodded to the nearest srinjid and the song began to die away. *Perhaps,* he thought, *I should not have made them sing. The Inquestor will be sad.*

"More sad than you can imagine," the Inquestor said, as though he had heard Toléon's thoughts. "You don't know how their city was annihilated. You cannot understand Arryk's rage at my love for a shortliver."

Toléon still avoided the Inquestor's gaze, but he could sense that he was looking away. He dared to look up a little.

The Inquestor was looking at the whisperlyre, that relic, that object of occasional worship, locked in a dome of force. Presently he ordered the old man to unlock the dome.

Toléon muttered a subvocalization that may not be revealed, and he was able to reach in and touch the relic. It has strange, he thought, that he had never touched it in his life. There was a kind of tension behind the field; when it dissolved, dust seemed to settle on the instrument, where before it had been suspended in a quasi-vacuum. He brought the instrument to the Inquestor, kneeling to present it. When Elloran touched it, there came a wheezing, jangling sound and a sudden rainbow flash that dissipated into a white mist.

"You should leave us, perhaps," said the Inquestor.

And Tash Toléon saw that the godlike being was weeping. "An Inquestor—"

"Does not weep!" Elloran said softly, yet did not cease to weep. "Do you still think I am what you thought me?

Do you not know that I have cast aside my power, given away the worlds I owned? Even Varezhdur is not mine; I gave the palace that sails through space to Ton Siriss; I travel by Varezhdur only through her grace, because she did not want me completely cut off from the life I knew."

Toléon saw that the old Inquestor could not be comforted, certainly not by a Remember's words. So, as unobtrusively as possible, he left; and there he was, an old weeping man in shimmercloak, on a stool on a lonely planet, clutching an instrument that had not played in a century or two.

***

Subjectively he was no more immortal than any of the trillions of the timebound. Yet Elloran had spent so much time in the space between spaces that to a man such as this Rememberer he must have seemed eternal. How often had he travelled from one world to another, to return and find the first world *fallen*

beyond?

Even so, as his hands held the leathery frame of his old friend's whisperlyre, he could imagine what it was like to live in little steps, to grow old, to die, in a heartbeat. Those moments were a heartbeat away. *The meeting in the bowels of a doomed starship. The journey to find the Rainbow King, and the hunting of the first utopia. The voyage to the world of the dust-sculptress, who love dust more than she could love an Inquestor.* And all those momentous events framed in the songs of Shen Sajit.

My life was lived in earshot of Sajit's great poetry, Elloran thought. *Sometimes all Varezhdur resonated in sympathy to the plucking of a single string of the whisperlyre.*

He moved his hand over the strings. Only a jangle came forth. He touched the fingerboard, still sensitive; it responded to the slightest change in pressure with a cascade of color, for, like the shimmercloak he wore, it was on some level a conscious being. It knew that the one who touched it was not Sajit.

***

... a bone-thin boy, laughing ...

The streets of Aírang, city of pleasures. Turning a corner. The smell of mulled *zul* from an unseen alley. Dancing pteratygers in the sky, images woven by giant dreamweavers clamped to the tops of minarets ...

Elloran stirred. It was one of the images that came to him often now, though it could not be a true memory. So often Sajit had spoken of growing up in the streets of the pleasure city. But Elloran had not known Sajit in those days. Only later, when they had come together, in adulthood, to forget things that cannot be forgotten.

The whisperlyre clattered on the flagstones.

Blurred light. A buzzing sound. The strings, perhaps, or insects of the night. Then the servant of the shrine, that fawning Rememberer, was back, with a tray of fruit and pastries.

"Forgive me, hokh'Ton. I know you requested aloneness, but...."

"Yes, yes. Where does one lodge in this village?"

"There is an Inquestral guesthouse. It has never been used."

"We shall go there."

"But first, hokh'Ton, there is something I must tell you."

"You have something to tell me? Curious."

"Yes, Lord. For the whole Dispersal knows that you knew Sajit as you know yourself. And the whole Dispersal knows the stories and calls them true: songs about them are sung, actors play the bard and the Inquestor in operas, in servocorpse dramas. We know of the hunting of your first utopia, of the pursuit of the woman in the dust, of the building of Shentrazjit and creation of the srinjid symphony; of Sajit's death and Arryk's rage and of your grief that lasted a century and more. And it is known throughout the Dispersal of Man that one day you come to this village and sit in front of this shrine."

Elloran listened, for the last sentence he had not heard before. And now he listened intently.

"I was given the duty of waiting for you, said Toléon, as was my father before me, and *his* father. Because of this duty, my grandfather elected not to be taken up into a people bin when our world was selected to *fall beyond*. And he waited in this sanctuary, knowing one day you must return."

"And I have," Elloran said. "But what must you tell me?"

"I must tell you, hokh'-Ton, that everything you ever knew about Sajit was ... inaccurate."

"Do you mock me?"

"Never, my Lord. But you must believe me when I tell you that when you crossed the world of the dead to confront the heretic Inquestor, the one who shared your journey was not Shen Sajit. When you quarreled over a woman, your rival was not Sajit ... or, perhaps, he was, but at times he was not. It was not Sajit for whom you made the singing city, nor Sajit whose body you sent there, swooping down in his golden hearse, to be interred in song. Sajit lives, though he does not live. You shall see him again, you shall see him yet you shall not see him. Because, Ton Elloran n'Taanyel Tath, I am here to be the memory you never had. I am here to speak of the Sajit you never saw. Because, my Lord, there were *two Sajits.*"

***

And thus it was that Tash Toléon began to speak of a boy named Sajit. And because he was a trained Rememberer, the boy sprang to life in the telling, and Elloran saw everything he thought true torn up, sundered, reassembled into another truth.

"Once upon a time," he began, "the name of this world, which now has no name, but only a set of coordinates, was Alykh, and it was a planet of great pleasure cities. In this city an orphan beggar boy named Sajit lived, singing in the marketplace with a broken whisperlyre, until one day ...

"Ah, but before that pleasure planet, in the same coordinates, there was a world named Urna, a world of few pleasures, and fewer cities; mostly there were villages, tiny, impoverished. And in one those villages there lived a boy named Sajit"

***

So the telling began. To hear the Rememberer's voice was to gaze into a mirror with no edge, and to see the mirror mirrored and re-mirrored, unto infinity.

And the mirror of the mirror's mirror was the soul's soul's soul.

One
Attembris

A chill gray space....

A pool of light in a deep dark forest ...

In the dream it is always the same, the same circle of attenuated starlight, the same musk-drenched odor of *vanjeris* leaves, the same breeze, barely felt, bearing the scent of a lost city. And the singing moons.

The place can be visited only in dreams because like so many places he has known, it has *fallen beyond* in the great game that is played between those near-immortals whose caprices control the destinies of the million worlds of the Dispersal of Man. And when a world has *fallen beyond*, it lives only in song, and song belongs to the poets alone.

But oh, oh, oh, the poet cries, I want to enter that circle once again, to touch the silky strands of the *vanjeris* and see the rosella petals dancing in the breeze, in the column of chill gray light. And he dreams again. And dreaming he returns always to this place....

The place he dreams of is just outside the village of Attembris. And where is Attembris? you may well ask. For the place does not live anymore, not even in song and story. Yet for one man it is the very center of his homeworld, the homeworld of the heart.

The village itself was barely deserving of that name, being a mere cluster of houses around a displacement plate that linked to the central square of a slightly larger village, whose square in turn was linked to that of an abandoned temple. Abandoned, for religion had not been in vogue for some centuries.

Once, when he was much younger, he had set foot in

that temple. That's where he first saw the woman cloaked in shadow.

The way she looked at him ... she was close to him ... in a way that even his own mother was not.

"Who are you?" he asked her.

But she did not answer, and indeed, when he looked again, she was gone.

From time to time, he dreamed of her.

***

Their house was the last house in the village, just outside the gate. The gate opened out onto a pathway, but that pathway was subsumed in moss and weeds, for pathways too were no longer in fashion since the network of displacement plates had become operational.

From the boy's bedroom, the forest was but a single step away. Thus, darkness and mystery were always within his reach.

Since he could barely walk, he had learned to go there when he was afraid, or when he simply needed to be alone. He had learned to count the thickets until the spaces broadened and there was a ring of stones, perhaps made by men, or left behind by the Inquestors, perhaps even from the time before there were humans in this world.

When he came to this place, he could always hear the music. Especially when at least three of the moons were full. It seemed to him that the moons could sing. It was a manystranded singing. Each of the moons had a separate voice. They sang in a pure and absolute harmony, making chords that he had never heard from the village choir, when they met each tennight to sing the *Dhelyá Sarnáng,* the anthem to the High Inquest.

And what did the moons say to him?

They said: *You are not who you think you are. You are a different person. This is not your world.*

It was only when he was a little bit older, that he realized the singing came from within his own mind. That other people did not hear the music the way he did. And that he could reproduce that music at times, making new sounds that the world has never known. He could pluck the sounds from his mind and make any instrument repeat them, whether it was the panorchestrion in the village square or the old whisperlyre that had been his grandfather's, or even a bunch of twigs and an ystrell skin stretched over a jar. They called it a gift.

Because of this gift, they told him, we have to protect you. You cannot be called the way other children are called. We're going to have to find a way to hide you when they come for you.

"But why will they come for me? Who are they, that I must be so afraid?"

"You don't need to know that yet." That somehow always ended the conversation.

For the world that the boy lived in was a safe world that had few terrors. Children were not afraid. They played all night and knew nothing of demons, ghosts, or vile spirits. On the whole, the people of his world were warm and openhearted. It was not a world that had frequent wars or conflicts. In a way, it was a world that verged on Utopia.

But the boy learned very young that the word utopia was not to be uttered. It could not even be thought. For the edge of utopia was a good thing, but beyond that edge lay annihilation. A utopia would always, one day, *fall beyond.* The boy had learned in school that "the breaking of joy is the beginning of wisdom." Everyone knew that.

He may have been too young to wander around in the forest late at night, but there were times when he could not help himself. They were the times of strange, disturbing dreams; of twisting and turning; of wondering about the things that the adults would not speak of.

In the night, in the forest, in the clearing, by the gray misshapen boulders, in the light of the dancing moons, that was music. That night he heard the music so clearly that he thought a visiting *klazmurah* might be in the vicinity. They did come to the village from time to time, on the way to a bigger city, to a princeling's court, even on the way to the residence of the High Inquestral Legate. But no. There was no one else there. This music was in the air itself, was woven from strands of the shifting moonlights, and the wisps of mist. And yet, he could even pick out a line or two of melody, weaving in and out of the unearthly harmonies.

He could almost hear the words.

And before he knew it, the words were leaving his lips, words barely understood, yet fully formed.

Den Táthes eyáh
Den Sírana.

The words he formed were words of the High-speech, a language no one spoke, but which you had to learn in school. He sang about the trees and the wind and the dancing moons; the intertwining harmonies he heard enveloped him, buoyed up the song with its meandering melismas. Surely this was an ancient music such as might be heard streaming from a malfunctioning song cube.

It is neither the winds
Nor is it the moon....

"That is true," said someone. "It's you, just you alone."

The rest of the song died on his lips. Suddenly the woods and the air were silent, and the light was only light.

"Who's there?"

"What do you mean, who's there?"

Nothing is dangerous on this world, the boy told himself. He turned. The clearing was empty. The ancient boulders ... were they glowing a little?

"Come out and show yourself," he said, trying to sound like his father. "My parents are important in Attembris. I don't scare easily." By now he was very scared indeed, and eyeing the escape path anxiously.

The forest laughed.

The laughter, like the music before it, seemed to come from the very air, from the rustling leaves, from the branches stirred by the chill wind. And then the boy saw its source: a man was e-merging from the shadows between two trees. As he materialized, he went on laughing. Finally he seemed to notice the boy's dis-comfiture.

"I'm so sorry," he said. "I forgot that I was invisible. It's easy to forget to turn the thing off. In the city, one becomes used to being invisible."

"I'm not afraid," said the boy. "I was just startled. Where I come from, people don't just appear out of thin air. It must be a city thing. Is this your land? I'm sorry! I shouldn't be out here."

"And why not? On a night like this, in a lit clearing beneath the Dancing Moons of Urna, a sight well celebrated in song and story?"

"What are those words I sang? Is it an ancient song I learned and somehow forgot until tonight?"

"Not at all," someone said. "It's completely new. And miraculous."

The man laughed again. He was not old, not young. He wore a simple wrap cloth over one shoulder. His kilt was gray. You had to look closely to realize that it was handwoven, and that the belt was a living, opalescent serpent with red eyes, and a forked tongue that flecked the man's bare midriff, perhaps enjoying the salt in his sweat. Yes, a casual glance would have revealed nothing, yet here, in the light of the dancing moons, given the fact that he possessed a privacy shield, which would have cost his father a year's salary, the boy knew that this was no ordinary villager who happened to be taking a walk in the woods.

"Are you a senator? A counselor? A Princeling?"

"Princeling!" The man laughed again. "My, what big eyes you have." But Sajit saw a big lapis ring with an intagliate design of mating serpents, and sensed that it was the insignium of an important family.

"I've learned all the formal modes of address," the boy said. "I never thought people actually used them."

"And who, then, are you, who fill the forest with such haunting melody that even I, who stop for nothing, should stop to listen and to know, should pause invisibly in this wood to hear him?"

The boy looked into the man's eyes then, and knew that this meeting was the most important moment of his life. In school, his classical tutor Arbát had taught him that lives are journeys and there are cross-roads on those journeys and on these crossroads one may meet a traveler one would never meet on one's own road. And these travelers can change lives. This traveler was one such, he knew it. "You're going to change me," he said.

"You are wise," said the man, "to say something such as this to a man whose name you not even know. And who does not even know your name."

"My name? Nobody asks my name. I'm too young to have a name, really. But in the village I am called Sajit son of Areon darSajit the keeper of the village think-hive."

"Then I greet you, Sajit-without-a-Clan. You shall hear from me again. And in the meantime, I give you this gift."

And plucked a sound cube out of the empty air. Tossed it to the boy. In the light of the dancing moons, it seemed almost alive.

Sajit squeezed the sound cube in his hand, releasing the hidden music. Sounds poured out. Such sounds! Oh, he had heard the wind singing. He had heard the melody that streamed from the intertwining of the light of all those moons, the dark ones and the pale. This was different. It was perhaps rooted in nature, but it was far from natural. This music has been *composed*.

Which meant that he did not come from some village tunesmith, but from an artist of one of the great courts.

Sajit wanted to thank the man, but he already disappeared. Perhaps he was still there, but if so he had switched his privacy shield back on. So Sajit sat for a while letting the music play, not daring to sing again for fear that someone was eavesdropping. For even then, even as a child, he knew he did not want strangers to hear his songs until they had become perfect.

And so he allowed the strains of the artificial music to seep into his very being, and slowly he drifted back into one of those strange dreams, the ones had been having all year, the one about starships and exploding planets and the long cold silences between the stars.

And amongst the stars, there stood a woman cloaked in shadow, and he was whispering, "Tell me who I really am."

•••

When he woke, it was already morning, and he knew he would be in trouble. He made his way home in a great hurry, barely lingering at each displacement plate. Even so, he arrived at his bedroom window too late to be able to climb back in discreetly. The family servocorpse was already bustling about the room, folding up the bed so it could be put away in the drawer, and injecting the lamps with glowworms. Luckily the servocorpse was not an intelligent model, and would be telling no tales.

But when he reached the breakfast circle, the whole family was already gathered, and the morning meditation seemed to have been interrupted.

"Mother, I —"

Ina desAreon put a finger to her lips and turned to Sajit's father.

Usually, Areon darSajit was taciturn in the mornings. But this time Sajit's father spoke. "I don't think it's necessary for us to ask where you spent the night, my son. Whatever happened, you seem to have brought our family immense favor."

Sajit looked at the center of the breakfast circle. There

was a globe. It glistened. It floated above the ground by some fancy antigrav mechanism. The globe carried the seal of the Senatorial House of Urna.

"We are asked to keep the contents of this globe a secret," his father said, "but I think it only fair to tell you that it is a doppling kit."

"But they only make those for the Royal Family!"

"Exactly. We have always said that we must find a way to hide you if the time were to come, and the means has suddenly been provided, and by the highest provider on this planet."

"We are proud of you, son," said Ina, "even though we don't quite know you pulled it off."

Sajit looked at his mother and father, then at his two younger sisters Chanika and Vimla. Nobody answered him. It was clear that the honor was so unprecedented, so exalted, that it was almost beyond comprehension. Whoever the man was, he had deemed the boy Sajit so important that a clone would have to be made, and that

clone kept hidden away just in case the Inquestors came.

Sajit, of course, never seen an Inquestor. To see one when is rare as to be visited by one of the gods of the ancient religions. He spoke their language of course; everyone had rudiments of the high speech in school. And he had learned a little of their history from his classical tutor, although the history of the High Inquest was not a regular subject for a village school.

He knew that they came only once in a decade or two, sometimes only once in a century. But when they came, they always took away the children. For far away, on the other side of the mysterious overcosm, wars were being fought, planets destroyed, worlds were falling beyond in an eternal dance of creation and destruction. And wars demanded children. Only a prepubescent child, his reflexes honed to the utmost, could manipulate the streams of deadly light from implanted laser-irises. Even after millennia of human invention, the child was still the most efficient killing machine in the Dispersal of Man.

The presence of a doppling kit in the house meant two things. One: Inquestors were coming. They were probably coming very soon. The comings and goings of the High Inquest were known only to the Senatorial Council. Two: the preservation of Sajit of Attembris was of crucial importance to someone in a very high place.

Doppling kits were of course forbidden. Even natural twins were taboo in some villages, and one would be selected for a painless devivement, to prevent a-bomination. *Doppling is against nature,* that was a precept everyone repeated in school. *The individual can be but one.*

But there are some people in this world as in every world to nothing is forbidden.

Ina looked at the artifact with both exhilaration and dismay. "It's a curse," she said. "But it had to happen.

One way or another. We always knew."

But his father said, "Perhaps we need to see this in a better light. Perhaps we should see this as an emblem of hope. If the Inquestors are truly coming, many families in the village will shed tears. But our family may not. There is opportunity here, opportunity as much as risk. Sajitteh, how old will you be come summer?"

"I haven't been counting, father." The morning *zul* was getting cold. "My teacher says I'm too busy dreaming to count the years."

"Next year, he will be ten," his mother said. "Twelve and it's too late, we'll be safe."

But if they are this concerned, Sajit thought, *we must not be talking about next year.*

They ate in silence for a long time. Sajit wondered when they were going to start up the doppling kit, but no one mentioned it. That day, when he returned from school, it had already been put away somewhere, and he dared not ask where.

***

That night again, he dreamed of the woman cloaked in shadow. She stood beside his bed. In the dream, he said to her, "Are you my mother? Because ... sometimes I don't think these people are my real family." He thought he saw her smile before her whole face vanished once more into shadow.

***

And the next day he had no time to think of doppling kits, because he had been summoned to the Palace of a Thousand Snows, and his entire family with him. Even his tutor Arbát had been hired away from the village school and assigned to Sajit alone.

They brought almost nothing with them from the old home. But one thing they did bring. It was something from an old closet, something he'd never seen before ... pieces of an old whisperlyre.

"We'll hang this in a place of honor," Areon said.

"Yes," said Ina. "To remind us about ..." But she stopped herself.

Something was being kept from him. A piece of a puzzle. Like the woman in his dreams, like the man in the forest.

Of the summons from the palace, Sajit's father said only, "I used to think it was such a pity that you had no friends, but that too was a blessing. When we left Attembris, you had no one to weep over."

Two
Nevéqilas

Nevéqilas blossomed in the sky, a crystal chrysanthon on a glass stalk that stretched far above the minarets of the city of Shírensang, the Inquestral seat of Urna. It was a small provincial seat of only a million souls; the reach of its demesne was only a single world, one inhabited moon, and a few colonies dotting the sparse empty space between world and moon. Still, it was the biggest city Sajit had ever seen.

Sajit's family were lodged not far from the crystal stem that led up to the palace. It was so close, in fact, that there was no displacement plate connecting it to the square; it was about half a klomet to walk, down a real street with paving stones, not weeds, lined with shops, even; the brief walk was like a journey into a fairy tale.

The apartment was not a pretentious one, but compared to their home in the village it was in itself palatial. Each of the siblings had a separate room, and there was a music room which was connected to his own bedchamber. The breakfast circle was surrounded by simulated forest, so that they were always linked to Attembris.

They hung the broken old whisperlyre on a branch of the holosculpt tree of the simulated forest, and sometimes it swayed in a simulated breeze and let forth a simulated sighing.

There was another apartment, in a slightly poorer neighborhood, for the tutor as well; in fact though Arbát lived alone there, he had almost as much room as Sajit's entire family. Arbát's lodgings were further from the palace; it took a few displacements to get there.

Sajit assumed that on coming to the metropolis he would immediately be summoned into the presence of the mysterious lord who had discovered him; in fact, Arbát informed him, that was not going be happening soon ... not in a month, a year, or even *ever,* for the lord had, it was rumored, many protégés, each one kept carefully isolated from the other.

Instead there was going to be *training.* Training of a kind unimaginable in Attembris.

There was going to be some kind of routine now; whisperlyre lessons, the history of the clan of Shen, the great poets' clan, to be memorized, although Sajit could not dare to dream of one day being inducted into it himself; and formal instruction in the arcane theories and philosophies of music. And regular meals.

In the breakfast circle there were four double-purpose cushioned benches such as families use to store their belongings. Three of the benches contained eating utensils and dishes and a decorative light sculpture that would be used as a table centerpiece when the tutor, or other guests, would come for breakfast. The three benches opened easily with a subvocalized command. The fourth was always locked and Sajit thought better than to question this. His parents had many secrets.

Everyone had secrets. To be a child was to be kept continuously in the dark, to be told that such and such would be known "in due course" or "at the right time." The locked storage bench was one such mystery.

He did not question it until his curiosity got the better of him....

Which happened within a single tennight.

•••

His parents had gone to the corpse depot to find more adequate help, as the primitive servocorpose they had brought from the village would never be able to maintain a city dwelling properly. Corpse depots are soulless by their very nature, and never a favorite haunt of the boy's.

The whole family had gone, but Sajit was to see Arbát for a discussion of transstellar monody; it was a dull subject, and when Arbát's messenger arrived to say that Arbát would be indisposed for the day, Sajit was glad of the relief.

He was alone in the dwelling for the first time, and he thought about the locked storage bench.

He knew he should not think about it, but he could not help himself.

For an hour he entertained himself by practicing scales on a mnemokitharon, an instrument designed for discipline, not music; one had to play each scale correctly, at the right tempo, and in every permutation from direct through to inverse through to retrograde; a wrong note was rewarded with an unpleasant tingling, like an insect bite.

It wasn't long before Sajit found himself wandering back to the breakfast circle. And gazing at the four storage benches, of which only one was locked — the one he himself usually sat on every morning.

He knelt down and knocked on it. The material was natural, some kind of old wood. That in itself was curious; organics had been passé for decades.

He knocked.

Knocked harder, laughing.

From inside, something knocked back. His heart skipped a beat. *It's haunted,* he thought.

Sajit ran to his room. He couldn't wait for his family to get back, and he babbled all through the next meal, boasting of the scales he could play.

•••

The new servocorpse was a talking model, but of a rustic demeanor and limited vocabulary. They decided to call it Bo, even though the naming of servocorpses is fraught with danger, for one might come to think of them as people. Bo was not a friend, but in Nevéqilas Sajit had not yet found friends. So it sufficed.

Days more passed, in the company of Arbát mostly. A classical music education mostly begins with the mnemokitharon, and the memorization of long sequences of scales, as well as the philosophical, historical and emotive basis of each. Each of the four hundred and seven divisions of the octave had a name, and the notes were classified by color as well as by the degree by which they bent away from the thirteen basic tones.

And Sajit, you knew all these things by instinct, who grasped the roots of music with such ease, found the naming tedious, and wished always to get to the creative part of the lesson, often delegated to the last few minutes. It did not take long for Sajit to understand that he was more gifted than his teacher.

Arbát was also something of a dreamer; often Sajit could smell the dreamstuff on his breath, and often Arbát drifted into a reverie, as he had consumed too much. He was, Sajit realized, bitter — though why, it was hard to know, since he had now been rewarded with such great fortune, a city dwelling, a stipend, and only a single pupil to teach.

Unless it was his pupil's talent that made him bitter....

But Sajit did not want to consider this as he practiced the scales on the whisperlyre over and over, memorizing the assigned affect of each scale and the list of nuances of each subdivision, while Arbát stared into the middle distance, pausing now and then to place an admonishing finger upon Sajit's fret-matrix ... "No, no, the second *dha* in the scries should be

flatter ... flatter ... listen harder won't you...."

The days went by and Sajit was home alone again, and his thoughts returned to the storage bench. And once again he crept into the breakfast circle. And knocked on the old wood. Which knocked back. He tried a cross rhythm he had just been practicing, his left index finger tapping fives and sevens while his right hand hit fours with the edge of his palm.

The same rhythm, very faint, came back at him from deep inside the wood. And in his dreams, that rhythm came again.

•••

... and there would come the dream again, and more fragments of the song ...

It is not the wind
It is not the moon ...

The words were becoming more clear now. But why only a single moon?

The snow is aflame,
yet the heart has frozen.

I am not I.

The words were of flaming snow, and a single moon. This was not Sajit's world. But Sajit had never seen another world.

In the dream, too, he would see the storage bench ... the box. And he knew they were linked.

***

One night he woke, and knew, somehow, that he *must* find out what was in box. He felt this knowledge inside himself, as though something in the storage bench were calling out to him, knew his name, even. It must be some kind of musical instrument, he thought, something powered by a microthinkhive so dense it could predict his very thoughts.

The family quarters were equipped with amnio-hammocks, not a luxury available in Attembris. The first time when he awakened and did not find himself inside a concrete world, but softly enfolded in a virtual, viscous fluid whose scent hinted of "mother" and "safety", he had not wanted to subvocalize the command to dissolve the hammock; this time he woke and snapped right out of the dream-world. Naked, Sajit dissolved the bedroom doorway with a half-uttered word and crept down the corridor to the breakfast circle. The storage bench was glowing.

He knelt next to it. A thought struck him: *It's the size of a coffin, a childsoldier's coffin.*

Because when the Inquestors came to cull the children, that was also the time when the coffins came home. Sajit wondered if there was some kind of servocorpse inside, perhaps one with a special synthesizing module; Arbát had hinted that such technology could be used to eke out the ensemble when an artist from the Clan of Shen performed solo in an Inquestral court.

Eagerly, he put his ear to the wood.

When his flesh touched the surface, the glow became brighter. Sajit tapped another rhythm, and heard the same rhythm echo back from within the wood. He put his lips to the bench and sang something he had just learned a few sleeps before, a song called *The Space between Spaces....*

I sing of the place
where stillness is rock
and where hardness is
the empty air;
I sing of the overcosm.
From inside came an
answer:
I sing of the place
where light goes mad
and where songs have no
endings.

"Who are you?" Sajit cried.

I am you. I am you. The melody arced and swayed with an overpowering sadness. It came from inside himself and outside himself at the same time. He found himself weeping.

Something was stirring in Sajit's soul. There had always been an emptiness in that deepest place, but he had never realized quite how empty it had been. *I have always been lonely,* he thought. Those nights wandering in the forest — he had been looking for something. For someone who might say these very words: *I am you.* What could be inside this cold wooden box that could awaken such feelings? Sajit hugged the hardness, trying to infuse into it the warmth of his own nude body. He felt something huge and powerful seize hold of him, like the wind from a burning star; he trembled; he shook; he cried out. It seemed that the wood was responding ... softening ... that he was sinking into it. That could not be. It was a just a box, a wooden box.

But the box was dissolving, and his arms were closing around a human form. a gelatinous foam clung to it. His lips found other lips. His eyes gazed into another's eyes. The foam was dissipating and he was pressed against someone whose body, cold at first, was catching fire from his body heat, starting to move, starting to return the embrace. The amnio oil that still clung to his limbs conjoined with the foam from the living thing within, as though the two fluids had the same genetic signature. Sajit gasped. He did not dare open his eyes. The creature from inside was thrusting against him, generating a warmth he had not felt except in dreams ... the dreams he dared not speak of ... loin to loin and lip to lip until without warning there came an explosion of feeling, much like singing a high note that is perfectly in tune, or playing a chord on the whisperlyre that resonates and resonates and resonates and never seems to leave the thick moist air.

Now lips at last broke free. At last bodies separated just enough for a puff air to pass between them. Sajit opened his eyes.

And saw himself.

Himself, as in a mirror. Slender hips, slender lips; slight, wiry, wide-eyed.

"I often dream of meeting myself," Sajit said.

"And I have dream ... of you," the strange boy said, forming words slowly at first, but then with growing confidence. "I dream of you as I lie in the dark foam, in the land where only dream is real."

Sajit sat straight up. "It wasn't myself I dreamed of then. I think I dreamed about you, too," he said, realizing it only for the first time.

"I hungry," the other boy said. "No. *Am* hungry."

Sajit realized know what the secret wooden box must have been. They had started up the doppling kit. A hair, a scab, an eyelash, a drop of blood is enough to get it going. His parents had been growing another Sajit.

"That was..."

"Surprising." The other boy had finished the sentence.

"Why," said Sajit, "you *are* me after all."

"Yes I am you," the other boy said. "I like what you do to me. When you put your arms around me and feels warm and cool at the same time. What is it?"

"I don't really know."

"I think I need food."

"I'll look."

As Sajit rummaged in the seats, finding a pouch of instant *zul* and a few small *peftifesht*, he thought, *So the Inquestors were coming after all.*

"Something to eat," Sajit said. He peeled the fruit and sprinkled the powdered *zul* over it. "What's your name? I can't very well call you by my own name." Then he realized how stupid he must found. Dopplings have no names. They are created only to die. They stand in for the real human being. And yet in every sense of the world they too are human.

"You must name me," the boy said.

Sajit looked into the boy's eyes, his own eyes. In the village, Sajit did not really have friends. Even his family were remote. He had the night. He had the moons. He had the secret music of the lonely night. He had always wanted someone. Someone to whisper secrets to, someone to cling to in the darkness. He never dreamed that someone would be himself.

"Tijas," he said.

His new friend smiled. "You name me after yourself," he said.

And Tijas stepped out of the womb that had also been a coffin. He waved his hand over the wood and it became hard once more. "It keys to our genetic code," Sajit says. "So you may command it as much as I may."

"Teach me things," said Tijas. "In the womb, I grow quickly. I not ... connect ... one thing with another."

"The first thing we'll teach you," Sajit said, "is there's more to life than just the present tense."

"No time where I come from."

And maybe, Sajit thought, *there isn't any time left for me, either.*

The Inquestors were coming. No world was ever the same afterwards.

But, Sajit thought, *I shall not be alone.*

•••

Tijas was Sajit's secret.

"You're not concentrating!" said Arbát.

"And why should I concentrate?" Sajit shouted, and

he began fingering the whisperlyre in a perfect sequence as he had been taught: *dha, dha, bent dha, double-dha, sharp dha, sharper dha, dha-ni dha-ni ni-ni-ni, dha, dha.* Not a note was out of place, every microtonal *shrut* was accurate to beyond the ear's capacity to distinguish, and Sajit knew it. "I can already play it perfectly."

"You can at that." Arbát sighed. "And yet perfection is not an end in itself, but a beginning. Listen, you stupid boy."

Sajit relaxed into the receptive pose called *savezhatá,* the locus of wisdom. His legs were crossed, sinking into the fur-cloaked floor. His palms were held out, cupped left and right, to receive the double stream of illumination that they said should come from the teacher, and the teacher's teacher and the teacher's teacher's teacher, all the way back to Shen Élumel, the mother of songs. He knew that Arbát would play and the sequences would be indistinguishable from what

he had produced, and yet he would be asked to hear the differences, and perhaps slapped around a bit if he could not come up with something, for what is the acquiring of knowledge without pain? So he entered the learning state, bracing himself a little in case his teacher was of a mind to strike him.

Dha, dha, bent dha —

But this time, it seemed to him that the notes touched him in a different way. The bending of the *dha* was the squeezing of teardrops. The nudge of the repeating *ni ni ni,* so close yet so far from the home key of *sa,* evoked in him such longing, a longing that was both dark and fiery.

Arbát's voice was reedy and worn. And yet within that voice was fire, and also history. He was connected to the dawn of music. Now, above the ostinato of *dha, dha, bent dha,* he began to sing, his tones setting off the whisperlyre's sympathetic strings and awakening the harmony globes within its mechanism. The words of the song were of love, of love between living stars, of the city built to memorialize the mutual suicide of twin stars that had once revolved around each other.

Unbidden, the image of Tijas surfaced. *Tijas!* Your eyes, my eyes! Your skin, my skin! Your touch, my touch! The confluence of sweat co-mingling with liquidescing amnio-wood, the eyes opening, the desire dredged up from an undiscovered darkness ... *Tijas!* For a moment he was afraid he had spoken aloud. But no. He had stopped himself in time, and yet....

Tijas, Tijas ... the whisperlyre whispered, the name surfacing from the the sussurator at its heart. Invading the texture of the song, lacing each harmony with soft scintillant esses.

Abruptly, Arbát stopped singing.

The whisperlyre's soundcolors became a jangle.

"A very good lesson for the day," said the old teacher. Sajit flinched without thinking, knowing a blow would come, but instead it was a tender stroke of the neck. "Never subvocalize your innermost thoughts when you are in the vicinity of a whisperlyre that is being played. You know that the instrument has a very sensitive thinkhive attached to its sussurator. It's there for a reason. The song is not just what you sing. It is what you are. And you have just revealed to me that you have a secret lover."

"Not a lover!" Sajit protested.

But Arbát merely wagged a finger. "Love comes in many forms," he said. "I told your parents they must not keep you locked away ... somehow you would find a way out. You would meet people. After all, that is how you came to be here in the first place. Your parents have to understand that you will go where you will go."

"Master, it isn't like that."

"Of course not," Arbát said, "I am sure I have all the details wrong. I don't know if this Tijas is a street urchin, or a kindly shopkeeper, or some mighty Lord or Lady you have run into in the corridors of your dwelling. But you feel what you have never felt before. Something that pulls from the deepest part of your unconscious mind."

"Yes, master."

"So what do you think of me now?"

"You're not as boring as you used to be," Sajit blurted out. Again, miraculously, no blow came. Indeed, his teacher smiled, something Sajit did not remember ever seeing before. His face was like the crinkled nets for catching phoslings in the double summer.

"I daresay," Arbát said. "Now, learn your lessons carefully. When you perform, you are the song. When the song bleeds, you bleed. When the song weeps, you weep. You must distill the universal from yourself; yet how to do so when *yourself* is still but an embryo? I am not here to create your path for you, but to provide a bare minimum of light so you can see your own."

Then came the blow, so sting-ing that Sajit clenched back tears. And yet, he thought, this pain is beautiful.

•••

That night, Chanika and Vimla quarreled, and the quarrel set off his parents. Sajit could hear them arguing into the night, and even when it all subsided, he could not sleep.

When he was sure no one would awaken (and when they quarreled, their sleep was usually deep) he dissolved the seal and pulled Tijas out of the storage box. The wood gave easily now, and hardened again when the boy was free of it.

"Come," Sajit said, "we should get you some clothes."

Sajit's room was bare, though one wall had a built-in imager which he had set to show a vista of the forest beyond Attembris. Set in a temporal loop, on a slowed down cycle, the imager had a sense generator. A wind wafted and you could almost feel its touch. Tijas said, "I know this. I've been there."

The moons were rising. In the distance — though the

wall held no real distance — came the wail and clang of an itinerant *klazmurah*. The honeyed, cloying scent of *vanjeris* hung in the moist air — though the room itself had been environmentally regulated and was quite dry and of a perfect temperature.

"I shouldn't be," Tijas said, "but I'm cold."

He was still naked from the doppling kit.

Sajit parted his amnio-hammock and pulled put a scrap of clingfire. He threw it to Tijas and it wrapped itself around his frail body. They sat at the edge of the amnio-hammock and watched the moons as they danced, and Sajit sang to his other self the song that he had learned that day, understanding it, perhaps, for the first time.

Tijas said, "I can't go back into that box. It's ... a coffin. I won't be alone anymore."

Sajit said, "Stay with me then."

"But people will find out."

"Not right away," Sajit said.

They leaned back against the amnio-hammock and it soon enveloped them both, and Sajit drew the darkness tight around them, enclosing them both. The warmth of the hammock radiated inward and they were safe as twins in a womb.

•••

In the morning, Sajit's mother said, "You seem to be eating a lot!"

Sajit giggled as he bit into his third *peftifesht*, because Tijas was standing in a doorway and no one was looking that way, making faces. "I've got to go," Sajit said and bolted to the hallway.

"What do you think you're doing?"

"Come on, it's my turn again." Tijas grabbed his doppling's half-eaten fruit.

Sajit hid to one side of the entrance and Tijas tiptoed to the breakfast circle. He squatted and went on eating.

"That was really fast," said Chanika.

"More zúl?" said Ina, waving to the servocorpse. "It'll get stuck in your throat."

Tijas nodded and Sajit sup-pressed a giggle.

"Make him sing for it," Chanika said.

"Yes! Sing!" Vimla said.

"Don't be silly, Chani, Villi," said their father, but Ina said, "Why not? You come back from the lessons and go straight to your room. We don't know what you and wicked old Arbát are cooking up."

"We don't need to know," said Sajit's father. "It's enough to know that because of Sajit, we have all this: a four-arjent income, a place in the capital in the shadow of the palace ..."

"We were not nobodies in Attembris," said Ina. "Sing for us, Sajit."

Sajit froze. Tijas had never had a singing lesson in his life. They would all be in trouble.

But Tijas closed his eyes and took a deep breath and began, repeating note-perfectly what Sajit had sung to him last night. First the melismatic sequence with the slippery microtones: *ha, dha, bent dha, double-dha, sharp dha, sharper dha, dha-ni dha-ni ni-ni-ni, dha, dha ...* then words, fitting to the serpentine melody as a shimmercloak bonds to an Inquestor's skin:

> *do chitáry mu eyáh*
> *mu eyáh élumy do*
> *káng késy eklissío*
> *kwan amby min eyáh?*

I never sang those words to him, Sajit thought. Yet they bespoke his innermost feelings: "I have two hearts. I have two souls. How shall I pull them apart when both are I?" He looked at his parents, who sat ensorcelled by Tijas's voice. How could it be that there was this other Sajit, conjured up from a wooden box? But there were other things Sajit realized as well.

His parents weren't happy about their new situation.

On some level, they resented him. He had brought them untold fortune, and now they were losing control, becoming bystanders in a larger story.

Sajit gestured, trying to catch Tijas' attention. On a high note, their eyes met, and Tijas's voice cracked a little. His parents seemed almost relieved that their sound had shown a touch of imperfection.

As the song ended, and its final notes still hung in the air, it would take a while for his family members to awaken from the rêverie that great music always induces. With the instinct of a showman, Tijas slipped delicately away.

•••

Back in Sajit's room, he said, "We fooled them!"

And Sajit laughed, but there was in his laugh a twinge of bitterness.

Before Tijas could ask him, Sajit said, "You know why."

"Yes, I do."

"We are each other."

"Soon I'll have to go back in the box."

"Yes, as soon as they leave the house."

"I don't want to."

"I know."

Sajit kissed his doppling ... himself.

Tijas said, "What are we doing?"

Sajit said, "I don't know, but I know that we have each other, and we've never had anyone before."

They kissed themselves again. Touched one another, fingertip to fingertip ... and felt the warmth-in-coolness that came in no other relationship.

"Tomorrow morning," Sajit said, "Let *me* go inside that box."

Three
Inside The Box

Darkness. A deeper amniosis than any hammock. A warmth that tingled first, then seeped, then overwhelmed. Darkness that is mother, all-loving, all-embracing.

In the darkness, Sajit began to dream, and the dreams were not history, but they were history.

For a doppling kit must produce not a brainless entity with the same DNA as its double, but also a mind, a set of memories, a schooling about the nature of things. Alone in the amniotic world, Tijas had been in school, with prefabricated packets of information seeping into his brain in the semi-sleep of this artificial womb.

For twenty thousand years....

A single world with a single sun. Many worlds with many suns. More worlds. More suns. A war between a million worlds. A ravaged galaxy. And then ... a single world ... a vast sphere that enclosed the great black hole the heart of the galaxy ... on which a million suns shone ... but where a klomets-high atmosphere scattered the light to a constant pearly radiance.

Fleeing her war, a lone woman comes to this world. The world, powered by a thinkhive so immense that its omniscience is indistinguishable from a deity's ... a thinkhive that has brooded for aeon upon aeon ... a thinkhive that has never encountered a conscious being apart from itself ... a thinkhive who is about to fall in love with the woman Vara.

A living world with all the knowledge in the galaxy ... a woman ... a love story ... the first Inquestors ... the harnessing of the deaths of suns to create tachyon bubbles ... the creation of the delphinoid shipminds, the union of the giant brains that flew through the sunless sound with the crystalline eggs of the farfellor to make great ships that could sail the overcosm and hold the galaxy within the grasp of a few human beings ... the freezing of history ... the hunting of utopias ... the whole story of the Dispersal of Man poured in through the synapse portals of the doppling kit. And Sajit learned more than he had ever done in the village schoolroom of Attembris, because the history he was learning now was the common or universal history, which is only taught to those who sail the spaces between spaces.

He learned of the decree that children should serve as childsoldiers, because only children have the quick reflexes to control the implanted laser-irises that can vaporize a pebble ... or a city ... depending on their focus.

He learned of the clans, brotherhoods that spanned the Dispersal, each with its own arcane rules, and how children could be named to a clan by an Inquestor ... though usually only if they could survive the harsh winnowing of the child-soldier years. The clan that even his master, Arbát, had aspired to but never attained, the clan of Shen, the master Songmakers of the High Inquest. The Clan of Tash, the Rememberers; Rax, the Web Dancers; Kail, the Star Pilots.

... and how all wars between worlds had been ended through the grace of the Mother Vara and the power of the cosmic think-hive of Uran s'Varek, the Inquestors' homeworld...

... how wars between worlds had been replaced by the game of makrúgh, which sustained the balance of the Dispersal ... how worlds could *fall beyond* and disappear from the

There was time, and no time.

***

In the time that was not time, Sajit stood in a circle of light. Around him voices were whispering:

History there is, and no history.

Just outside the circle of light, pitch-black. But here and there, a rustling sound and a brief glimmer of pink against blue ... shimmer-cloaks.

The voices ... always soft, always understated, yet behind the words, an unimaginable power, because the words were the Inquestral Highspeech ... the language of poetry and song ... the old tongue of the High Inquest, which normal mortals do not speak.

There is an old man's voice. There is the voice of a boy. There's a woman's voice, a laugh that cascades like falling water.

The words are too soft to understand clearly, but once in a while there is a word that surfaces. *Tekiánver* ... a tachyon bubble. *Náruvas nîkas* ... new worlds. *Abáchadand* ... the Falling Beyond.

He struggles to listen. He is eavesdropping on a game of *makrúgh*. The game is as mysterious as it is seductive.

There comes another voice now, breaking through the others; the clear voice of a boy no older than himself, he he speaks with the authority of one a thousand years old:

"Sing, boy, sing. Do not listen to our idle chatter."

And a song springs to his lips:

> *Den om verék en-tinjet*
> *In dárein shirenzheh*
> No man alive has touched
> The silence between the stars....

And he is thinking to himself: I wrote this. *I, a child from a backworld, have written this song which the whole dispersal knows.*

But not yet.

***

The box dissolved and Tijas was there again. And it was night, and the household was sleeping again. A view of the forest undulated against the wall as it sensed his wakefulness, and an artful perfume of night-blooms infused the room.

"How much time has passed?" he said.

"A day," Tijas said. "And your parents ... and your sisters ... they never knew."

"But isn't it dangerous?"

"How dangerous? We *are* each other."

"But ..."

He looked into Tijas's eyes ... his own eyes. He sees so clearly, he thought. And I do too.

"Oh, Sajitteh ... I've spent eternity inside the box ... drinking in your *youness* with every slow breath."

"But there are memories you don't have. Things that

were said to you. Places you went with them." Tijas couldn't know everything.

"Fortunate then that we'-re such a loner."

And Sajit saw that this was true. Only by having a friend had he discovered that he had no friends before. When he interacted with his family, they were *doing*, and he was observing. To be like Sajit to his family, Tijas had only to retreat into himself.

"Sajitteh ... I went to your Master Arbát today! I learned so much! The scales, the melismas, the orna-ments..."

"Did he realize?"

"How could he?'

"Did he hit you?"

"Yes, of course, of course. I can take the pain. I never used it feel pain before. It's a new thing to me."

"Don't be too eager. Me, I'm never very eager. Arbát is a bore." Sajit did not want to remember that Arbát, somehow, knew he had a secret friend. He did not to admit, either, how strange it felt that there was another Sajit sitting in his place, melting into *savézhata,*

drinking in the old man's knowledge. "The old man is a bore. We drift into another world when he speaks too much. The are universes beyond his universes. We have contempt for him sometimes."

"But we never let that show, do we?"

Sajit laughed. "We try not to."

"That mnemokitharon of his really stings," said Tijas.

"Y o u *d o n ' t* k n o w everything after all," Sajit said. "There's a way to neutralize the fine tuner. Then, when you play out of tune, make sure you yelp convincingly."

"But that won't help me learn to play...."

"That's what *you* think. The truth is, we are already better than old Arbát. Having to listen for your own mistakes will teach you to be better, more than any shocking mechanism."

"But Arbát has all the scales and melismas in his head, like an encyclopaedia," Tijas said "I can't remember them all."

"You already know them all. You just don't know what they are *called.*"

"Do you think he has seen your soul?" Tijas said.

And Sajit said, "Quiet, quiet."

***

It was Tijas who caught Arbát with the dreamstuff, and only because of his ignorance of a little thing. For though Tijas was wise in many ways, having sucked in knowledge straight from the memories of the microthinkhives embedded in the doppling kit, he was really only a few days old. Urna's peculiarities of etiquette sometimes eluded him; sometimes he did not understand simple words, because the language module was not always updated to the latest shifts in dialect and slang. But he was learning every day.

This is what he told Sajit that night:

I come for Sajit's lesson. But I'm early, and don't know I should not enter until the summoning-crystal in the doorway shifted from blue to red.

And since the door-guardian was not one of the models that could think for itself, it simply let him in. It even bowed, though, being the cheapest of servocorpses, it did not speak. Sajit laughed as they snuggled in the simulated forest. And Tijas went on:

"Where is Arbát?" I say, and the dead man merely indicates with a slight incline of the neck. And then I see — oh, what I see! — it is madness!

Arbát was suspended in the air; below him was a pocket varigrav box, and next to it a fumigator; a golden ball of dreamstuff floated in the steam. Arbát clutched something —someone—in his arms; it seemed at first like a large, flopping doll, robed in torn skins. Floating in the gravity field, Arbát savagely clawing at the mannikin, the grinding, cursing at it.

I hide behind a potted gruyesh plant, with its flapping filigree of purple leaves.

"Ah!" Arbát was shrieking. "You beast, you monster, you arrogant child!" His eyes were open, but not gazing at the real world; it was some fantasy conjured by the dreamstuff's vapors. He was thrashing about. He was partly naked; or rather, he wore a loose piece of clingfire that billowed about. His face was puffy, purple; he grunted, he groaned.

Then I see it: that Arbát's mid-air frenzy it's a kind of sick mockery of how me and my doppling cling to each other as we sleep in the warmth of the amnio-hammock.

Presently, Arbát seemed overcome by a kind of convulsion and began thrusting at the doll ... it was, Tijas saw now, a servocorpse. Convulsing as well, in a timid echo of Arbát's paroxysms. Arbát shuddering to some kind of climax and something flew off the corpse's face and landed at Tijas' feet ... and he saw that the corpse had no face at all.

The face was blank.

And, staring up at Tijas from the twisted stem of the gruyesh plant ... his own face, Sajit's face.

Tijas froze. The dermomask was sheer and slippery, and it started to bond to the plant, sensing organic matter. And at that moment, Arbát tumbled to the floor! The servocorpse flew one way and Arbát scrambled to grab the mask ... and saw Tijas ... and pulled him into the chamber by the scruff ... shaking and bellowing. "You! What did you see? How dare you enter?"

Tijas, terrified, began crying. And his teacher slapped him, over and over. Then stopped. Looked at his own hands in horror. "This will cost me everything. My livelihood. You uncivilized creature, didn't your parents teach you what a summoning crystal is for?"

Arbát began to weep. And his grief was more frightening than his anger. And though Tijas was sore from being slapped repeatedly — Arbát was not a small man — he could not help feel a kind of pity.

"I saw nothing, Arbát," Tijas said. "I've only been

here for a moment or two. For my lesson."

And the wonder of it was that Tijas no longer felt he had to call the master *master,* or address him by any honorific; what he had seen, though he did not really understand it, had diminished the grand musician.

"Sajitteh," Arbát said. "There are ... things ... you'll understand when you are older."

"Yes."

"No lesson today."

Tijas rose, thinking he should leave. Then he saw the servocorpse lying on its side in a corner of the room. It had, indeed, no face, and its body, too, was featureless. Though naked, it did not even have a gender. But its back was scarred with scratches and gouges. A servocorpse feels no pain; the centers for all human feelings are turned off when it is turned on.

A cheap toy, brought to life by imagination fueled by the fumes of dreamstuff.

"No lesson today, but ..." Arbát gathered the scraps of clingfire, strung them together to cover himself more completely. "But I will take you for some ... some chocolate."

Tijas followed Arbát out to the street.

***

The displacement plate was right at the door, so that one could go from this corridor to the next destination simply by subvocalizing a few coordinates, but Arbát sidestepped the plate; taking Tijas by the hand, he walked him down a stairwell and out through an alley.

Arbát said, "You do not always find the thing you want, Sajitteh, when you take the displacement plates." His gnarled hand held the boy's firmly. His manic actions seemed forgotten. They turned a few more corners and the smell of chocolate hung heavy in the air. There were stalls everywhere. Here a whirring contraption spun chocolate from powder into cobweb patterns; here a woman with three eyes was melting chocolate with a flametorch and drizzling it into pincushions of snow. Here a fondue with intoxicating dreamberries, the source of dreamstuff.

Arbát stopped in front of one stall, seemingly at random; the minder was a grinning, fat man with no hair. Two tripods rose for them to sit. Arbát ordered, a mushy brown paste sprinkled with dreamflakes, and for Tijas an icy, crunchy bowl of confections shaped like pteratygers.

Tijas bit off a wing. The liquid inside was sweet, but it had a pungent aftertaste. He waited. It was clear that Arbát wanted to say something. At last, his tongue loosened a little more by the flakes of dreamstuff, he said, "It's worse for me than for you, you talented little shit. You have a family of sorts, even though your friends are back in the village; chances are they were never really your friends anyway. Everyone I ever had is dead."

"Dead?"

"Mine was a world that *fell beyond*," Arbát said. "Before I came here. They chose me so the music of my world would not die."

"... and it hasn't."

"No, it hasn't. But *I* did."

"I see," said Tijas, though he really did not.

"I wish I could wring your scrawny neck, sometimes. I know there's someone you love. I only have the words, the melismas, not the truth of love. Can you blame me for wanting to—"

"I don't know what it is you want, Master Arbát," Tajis said.

"They are pleasure corpses," Arbát said. Tijas supposed it was by way of explanation. "You can print out the faces on any think-hive, any faces you want; they're cheap, these corpses, poor quality; perhaps they died in accidents, were disfigured, were diseased; so the servocorpse factory just grinds them to a blandness. Completely featureless. And then they can be anyone you want to love. Or hurt. But Sajitteh ... I would never hurt you too deeply. You are the thing I can never be, you see. I must love you for that."

Tijas said the one thing he knew Arbát wanted to hear. "You will never hear me speak of any of this, master. Not ever."

"And because you can hold it all inside yourself, you shall be Shen. Which I never became."

"When I attain it—I shall insist they make you one!"

And Arbát laughed bitterly. "When ... a stripling who's never *burst the milk-pod* says 'when, when' ... knowing his destiny already. ..." And called for a posset of crushed violets, perhaps to steady his emotions. "*Airos hokh'tásieh; ektáshila shi-klát,*" he added in the highspeech.

"Love is the great joy; the lesser joy is chocolate," Tijas said.

"Well learned!"

***

And that's how I learn that our teacher is addicted to dreamstuff, and that he has some kind of obsession with us, and that he acts out his obsession on a helpless little

pleasure corpse ...

"You have all the fun!" Sajit said, trying to reconcile this astonishing story with the Arbát he was used to. "Why couldn't this happen when *I* was with the master?"

"He ever bruise you this badly?"

" H e e v e r b u y m e chocolate?"

"But seriously," Tijas said, "something has changed."

"We have power now."

"Sajitteh, what's *bursting the milkpod?*"

"I don't know. I've heard that we're too young to understand."

"I'm going to ask mother and father, at breakfast."

"Who says you're the one having breakfast tomorrow?"

"I do, brother. Be quiet, now."

"Yes. They'll wake."

***

So, when he fingers blundered at the mne-mokitharon, Sajit declared that he wanted chocolate.

"Oh, you manipulator," Arbát muttered, "you shrewd little pteratyger cub."

But Arbát took him to the alley. And left him on the tripod, in front of the vendor, while he wandered off by himself. And in that moment Tijas slipped out of a side street. Too many people thronged about for anyone to notice them, shadowslim, flitting in and out; sensing each other's thoughts, they could switch in an instant, catching just the moment when no one was looking.

Tijas said to Arbát, "So what, Master Arbát, is *bursting the milkpod?* I have no one to ask."

"Try your parents," Arbát said.

A few minutes later, Sajit said, "So, Master Arbát, what exactly does *bursting the milkpod* mean? Is it the highspeech?"

"Little beast! Did I not tell you to ask your parents?"

"Did you?"

"Not five jipek ago. Either you are exceptionally forgetful for one so young, or there are two of you."

'Oh, you are a comedian, Master Arbát."

Thus it was that Arbát became no longer a martinet taskmaster, but a fellow traveller. A friend, even. And it was all because Tijas had walked through a door uninvited.

***

Mind you, he did not stop trashing the boy, or boys, rather. They accepted that; it was tradition. But often it was a perfunctory slap and a softpedaled tongue-lashing.

It was because of the occasional slap that the boys learned something new about each other.

Sajit had let Tijas go to the lesson one morning, because he wanted to sneak out to the palace bestiary. But he had not gone five steps across the square when he felt a sharp pain rip across his knuckles. He felt his left hand with his right, expecting a welt or abrasion, but there was nothing. He looked down and saw a red stripe, quickly fading. *We're more linked than I thought,* Sajit reflected. He needed to reach his doppling right away, to share this news. And so he run to the other side of the square and whispered the coordinates, barely noticing the displacements he passed, the Fountain of Unwept Tears, the Forest of Statues, the Street of the Servocorpse Factories ... he reached the entrance to the apartment and lurked in the hall, which was decorated with busts of the nobility, set on columns of azurite, their eyes sculpted from blue diamants. Eventually, he knew, they would emerge ... the chocolate ritual had become a regular thing. When they did, he motioned Tijas, who shouted, "I'll be there in a moment, Master, do not wait," and then he embraced Sajit, laughing.

"Oh, it's so risky, you, me, here, in the corridor — you never know which of the statues is a spy."

"All right," Sajit said, "Close your eyes."

Tijas said, "Why did you slap me?"

"I didn't. I slapped myself."

Tijas said, "You're right. This was worth the risk, coming here like this."

"We can play this game almost openly," Sajit said.

"We don't have to *pretend* to be each other."

"Slap yourself again! I want to feel it again."

***

At the chocolate stand, Arbát's absences became a ritual. And they became longer and longer, and when he returned, he was more distracted each time.

So the boys began following him.

Sometimes it was buying dreamstuff. For three gipfers you could buy quite a handful. But once, it was something else. It was hard to follow someone moving swiftly through the city via displacement plates; you had to leap on *just so,* in the split second when the the think-hive reset itself for the next passenger, and make your mind blank so you didn't not accidentally subvocalize a completely different command; *and* you had to avoid being noticed by the one you were following. It was only because Arbát moved so sluggishly, never looking around, that he was easy ti follow.

This time his destination was, ironically, the palace bestiary, it seemed. It was a public day, a crowded day, and the pteratygers were being fed. Arbát moved slowly, but he was purposeful; the boys would have liked to watch the feeding. The keepers released a flurry of firephoenixes into the air, and the pteratygers swooped and hovered, avoiding the flames in time to snatch the birds as the dived earthward, and all safely inside a sphere of force. The crowd gasping at every somersault that ended in a fiery kill. The boys tried not to stop and look to long.

"He's turned a corner," Sajit said. Arbát had slipped between two serpentine columns. The boys followed. Kept to the shadows. Which was wise, because they had stumbled into a royal council chamber, and seated on a hoverthrone was the very man Sajit had met, once, in a forest, in the village of Attembris, beneath the dancing moons, the moons that had seemed to sing.

And it was thus that Sajit finally learned the name of his benefactor, for Arbát prostrated himself in front of the hoverthrone and spoke the formula for greeting a member of the Royal Family of Urna: "Let me be as the dust beneath your feet, High Princeling, mightiest under the High Inquest, Starry Highness."

A Princeling? My, what big eyes you have!

In the forest clearing, a time not long ago, that could be counted in tennights, this man had been toying with Sajit all along. His parents thought this favor must come from a high senator, or a member of the aristocracy. But this was a higher personage altogether.

This was none other than the Son of the Starlight, the High Princeling Orifec z'Urnasi Tath, hereditary Lord of Nevéqilas, Commander of the World Entire, He Who Answers Only to the High Inquest.

"We have to get closer," Sajit whispered. "This is important."

The council chamber was an oval, and ringed with the serpentine columns; the stone hissed as it twisted, giving forth a faintly menacing music. But the hissing provided cover; they would move without making any noise, neither the rustling of tunics or the slipping of sandals on the marmáreon tiles. So they ended up crouching quite close to the throne, behind serpent effigies that twisted slowly, as though they were alive.

The High Princeling, as it happened, was speaking of Sajit.

"Progress, Arbát, tell me of progress."

"He is quick enough, Starry Highness. Too quick. But no discipline at all. Would as soon break the rules as learn them. I have taught him most of the major, minor, anterior and superior ragas, with the ways each tone can be shaded, and he parrots them well enough, and yet...."

"Arbát, there is little time. When you told me to wait in the forest, and watch for a lonely young boy—"

So the meeting was not by chance! Sajit thought.

"Starry Highness, he's definitely someone who has a great destiny. I've seen many take the path, and most more diligent, but this one already hears the silence between the stars."

"Keep at it, then, Arbát. They will be coming soon, and then everything is going to change."

"I don't know if he can be ready so soon, Starry Highness."

"He *must* be. Everything must go perfectly. Or we will lose ... *all this.*"

"I'd best going, my Lord. I left him sipping on a whipped chocolate confection at the Dromek Shiklati."

No sooner had Arbát shuffled away than the Princeling spoke again.

"Sajit-without-a-Clan, you can come out now."

Sajit tried to move, but suddenly the columns snapped, turned, and twisted around both boys, like living constrictors. "Let me go!" he cried. "I can't breathe!"

"Relax. Both of you. Breathe slowly."

The High Princess brought his hoverthrone sailing toward the colonnade. "You don't wonder then, that I don't need to be surrounded by guards."

Sajit cried out. And so did Tijas. And Sajit felt Tijas trying to breathe ... as much as he knew Tijas must feel his own choking.

Orifec clapped his hands. The serpents went limp.

"People think they are just marmáreon," said the High Princeling, "but they are actually dead pythonoids, fitted with servocorpse thinkhives, and coated with a dermolithic fabric that simulates marmáreon quite convincingly."

Sajit freed himself. Tijas prostrated himself. But Sajit, who had encountered the Princeling under such unusual circumstances before, could not bring himself to. He looked him straight in the eye. "You were behind *all* of this," he said.

Orifec said, "I suspected you'd unlock the doppling kit earlier than you needed to. You're not one for observing any strictures. See, even the doppling shows proper respect."

Tijas said softy, in perfectly modulated court language, "I am but the dust beneath your feet, Starry Highness." Of course; he had learned the protocols while he lay half-conscious in the amniosis.

"The question is," said the Starry Highness, "whether your parents know. Oh, get up, Doppel-Sajit. No one is watching us here."

"His *name* is Tijas," Sajit said hotly.

"Now that is a problem, Sajit-without-a-Clan. Dopplings have no names. They are not, legally speaking, people at all."

"Tijas is a person. He's me."

"I am a person. I'm him," Tijas said at the same time.

"That is true for now, but will it be true when the time comes? And that time will be soon, I fear. Come, I will tell you something. Climb up onto my hoverthrone, it's big enough for all."

He brought the throne down to the floor. Boarding it, Sajit felt warmth; the cushions were living matter, covered with the same membrane that coated the inside of the doppling kit. Sajit felt powerful, as if he was absorbing wisdom and cunning through its pores. "Not surprising," said Orifec. "We are linked to the central thinkhives of my palace, and through them to the world itself."

Sajit sat beside the Princeling, feeling surprisingly at home. But Tajis sat at the Princeling's feet. "You see, children," said Orifec, "already, you are not *entirely* each other. Doppel-Sajit has never met me. He is bound to act differently towards me. There are always going to be these little things. As time passes, your souls will disengage. At the moment it is fresh, it is as if even thoughts themselves can pass between you. Come."

He motioned with a finger, and a shield of force enveloped the throne. People would not be able to see inside; there was a photon scatterer in the throne and it would be visible only as a diffuse luminescence. "I'll give you the tour of Urna."

The throne rose into the air, The ceiling parted. "Doppel-Sajit, join us," said Orifec. "Be one with your twin for a little while longer."

The throne zigzagged through between the needles of the crystal columns of the palace, then went skyward. The sun of Urna, brooding and ruddy, hung low. Shírensang became a miniature. It was not a large city; it was a blip of color amid a landscape of purple-blue fields and black forests. At the horizon, against the face of the sun, was something black. It looked like a dark cloud. It was whirling. At this distance it was a mere smudge in the clear air.

"What is it?" Sajit said.

"It is," said the Princeling of Urna, "a window into our destinies. It is a doorway into the overcosm. Something is coming, children, something big. Something is going to come through that doorway. It is being prepared for now. My councillor-observers noticed it almost two years ago. It is growing fast now, a little every day. That's why, Sajit, you were summoned."

"In case something should happen ... to the Royal Family of Urna."

The Princeling did not speak.

"You want that our songs will not die," Sajit said. "You want a poet of your own."

"At first," said Orifec, "I wanted a plan, in case the High Inquest had a child-soldier culling. But maybe what is happening is even bigger. Maybe it's not the service of the Royal Family of Urna that is your destiny. It is true that I am all-powerful on this world. But above all worlds stands the High Inquest."

The throne swooped down into a city square and Tijas pointed: "It's Dromek Shiklati!" There indeed was the alley of chocolate below them and there was Arbát, looking very lost, wondering where is charge was.

"I'll drop you off somewhere close," said the Starry Highness. "And don't worry ... I won't tell."

Sajit realized that this must be one of life's lessons: to gain power over others, know a secret. And promise never to tell it. And make them live in terror that the promise will be broken.

***

And so it was that for the next few sleeps, they traded places often. Sometimes Tijas would receive a sharp rebuke when he could not reproduce a lesson Sajit learned. Sometimes Sajit would forget a promise he had made to his sisters. But as more days went by, such incidents became rare. The boys became more daring, sometimes substituting for each other when a parent looked away for just a moment. To their own amazement, they did not get caught. The game continued.

The boys relished the times when they could be together more or less openly. They had managed to get away with the whole charade for several tennights.

Once they both joined a family picnic by the Lake of Luminous Loons; when the flock of birds descended on the water and simultaneously went dark in their rhythmic mating ritual, one would dash behind a tree and the other would emerge. With Chanika and Vimla running in circles, and Bo the servo-corpse barely sentient enough to follow rudimentary commands, it was not hard to continue the deception.

Vimla said, "Sajitteh eats like a pteratyger!"

"Don't worry," their father said. "We can afford it now."

The loons descended, with cacophonous cries, a curtain of light and they called out to their mates, each with its own melody that could be recognized only by one other bird in the whole world ... the birds glowed, their phosphorescent feathers reflected in the lake, reflected back up to bounce down from the clouds ... so many moons had risen that though the Star of Urna hugged the horizon, there was brilliance everywhere ...

Then darkness! The flood of light, the wave of mating calls, suddenly stilled as the flock, thousands upon thousands, dived like a single darkweaving onto the surface ... striking the water with a thunderous thud, all at once, then ignited once again by the contact between feathers and the salts in the water, shaking off the drops of liquid as the mating calls began again, each loon catching fire from the next....

The boys switched places again, laughing.

The loons rose up from the lake once more. Their individual cries blended into a carpet of sound and one by one they began to glow. They laughed again. They were always laughing in those days....

***

It was possible to snuggle into a single amnio-hammock; the doppling box was more difficult, but Sajit and Tijas managed it by leaving it partially ajar. The womb was not built for two, but the skein of information paths woven by the micro-thinkhives that operated it had no trouble reproducing itself; self-reproduction was a doppling kit's reason for being.

And so it was that both boys became wise. Apart during the day, each night they imparted to each other all that had happened. Twins of artifice, they were more inseparable even than twins born naturally.

Even with the quarrelsome parents, the chattering sisters, and the sometimes tipsy, sometimes sadistic whisperlyre master Arbát, they were in a kind of paradise ... indeed, a utopia.

And utopias, by definition, must end —

For it is an axiom of the High Inquest that utopias may not stand. Man is a fallen being. No one could know what the smudge on the horizon portended.

***

Ektásiens kasséranda arkhá savézhas.
The breaking of joy is the beginning of wisdom.

Four
Outside The Box

The Princeling Orifec now sent an open summons to Arbát, that he should bring the apprentice Sajit-without-a-Clan to perform a private recital.

The chocolate sessions were put on hold. Each day came with dire lectures, finicky technical details, and the mnemokitharon set to the highest detail resolution *and* the highest voltage; the sparks blistered Sajit's fingers for several days until Tijas volunteered to take some of the lessons, and some of the pain.

So it was in fact Tijas, not Sajit, who ended up being escorted by an honour guard from their apartment to the highest minaret in Nevéqilas. For Sajit was not there when the guard came ... he had sneaked away to the market square, looking for a better tuning fork.

Mother, Father and the sisters were there, too, painfully overdressed; even Bo, the servocorpse, was in attendance, standing behind the girls and straightening their hair every few moments. Tijas had the vintage whisperlyre, an instrument more valuable than a household of servocorpses; incorporating a sliver, they had told him, from a tree on Uran s'Varek itself.

Perhaps Sajit would have been amazed at his family's attire, because Tijas knew that in all his life Sajit had never known his entire family to go to an event where they took the trouble to wear matching, spangled *shurongas*, with the emblem of the village stitched into the waistbands; Sajit probably did not even realize that his family possessed such clothes, but Tijas, having absorbed the layout of the family home via the house's own thinkhive, new that the clothes had always lain unused in an old closet, inherited from some anc-

estor. In any case, he could see they were looking very stiff; Areon darSajit, in particular, seemed uncomfortable, sensing more keenly than usual his loss of familial control since Sajit had unwittingly transformed the family's social status.

There was an anteroom. Tijas recognized the architectural style as the same one the boys had encountered before, with the encircling colonnade of marmoreal-skinned dead snakes. In the center of the room was a holosculpt icon of the Princeling, twice larger than life, standing in a circle of light, on a raised platform with four steps. Taking their cue from Arbát, the family genuflected to the icon.

Arbát said, "Starry Highness, may I present Areon darSajit, a thinkhive maintainer from your village of Attembris, and his wife Ina desAreon. And their daughters, Chanika and Vimla. And my student, Sajit-without-a-Clan."

"Come," said the icon, making a gesture toward the

golden displacement plate at its feet.

The family moved forward, but Arbát quickly said, "No. The command in the language of court protocol was in the singular. Even I dare not step onto the Conveyor of the Presence."

Tijas, who was still in the position of genuflection, rose. He turned back to look at the family. *I'm such an impostor,* he thought. He wished he were the one running through the marketplace now.

Arbát said, "We'll remain in the anteroom. If the Starry Highness wishes to address any of us from the sanctum, he will do so through the icon-surrogate, I am sure."

Ina said, "He's our boy, Master Arbát."

"I'll be fine ... mother," Tijas said, and stepped up to the golden plate. And vanished.

***

The room he found himself in was like an open lotus, perched atop the topmost minaret of Nevéqilas; the floor was of writhing, living crystal nematodelike creatures, thousands upon thousands, that cushioned the body; wherever one lay, they reshaped themselves into a couch, a footstool, an armrest. A banquet was laid out no the floor, and there were guests, all of striking physical perfection; most wore no clothes, but had pulled up pieces of the floor and draped them about themselves.

Above the chamber, the roof had been deopaqued, so they appeared to be under an open sky. Four moons swam behind sheer clouds. Seven more had yet to rise, and the smallest, Eríkion, was weaving in a complex dance between the three largest. Beneath the sky sat Orifec, and in front of him was Sajit, and Sajit was already playing a whisperlyre ... and this one not with a tiny sliver from Uran s'Varek built into its soundpost, but perhaps carved in one piece from the trunk of a millennial *tállisama* tree. How could two dopplings be allowed to be seen, openly, at a public banquet, a royal event? Surely this was the worst kind of abomination.

Orifec gestured. Sajit found the next cadence and finished with an elegant flourish. Tijas blurted out, "We're both here! Right in the open! Starry Highness, how?"

Orifec said, "Look around you, Doppel-Sajit. Who of my guests is eating?"

It was true. The guests ... preternaturally beautiful ... their bodies perfect, gleaming ... their motions were as choreographed as a play ... and when he listened to their conversations, he realized ... they were looped.

"Everyone here is dead!" Tijas said, in wonderment.

"Oh, yes," said the Starry Highness. "A ruler can ill afford to be surrounded by living courtiers. My father and uncles were all ... done in, you know. Even I am not entirely innocent." He looked away. "Come closer, Doppel-Sajit," he said. "I want to compare the two of you."

He pulled Tijas up and sat him on the throne next to him, and motioned for Sajit to do so as well. Diffidently, Tijas settled into the soft fabric. Orifec said, "Look at you. I can't tell you apart at all."

Sajit said, "There's a mole behind my left ear."

"Not mine," Tijas said. "The doppling process doesn't create any flaws."

"It will," said Orifec, "if you try use it too many times." He sounded as though he was remembering something.

Tijas wondered what Orifec knew about doppling kits. Royal families did possess the technology, he knew. Was Orifec himself a flawed imprint of an ancient ancestor?

"Starry Highness," Sajit said, "Why is it that you only live among the dead?"

"I've told you," said the Princeling. "People like me ... we live in mortal fear all the time."

Tijas said, "No, Starry Highness, there's more to it than that."

And Orifec became very quiet. A tear? But that would be unthinkable; weeping is for peasants. Orifec said, "You both sense it. I knew you would."

"What is it we sense?" said both the boys.

"One day, I may yet tell you."

Indeed, Tajis thought. *The doppling process....*

Orifec looked at both of them and Tijas could not understand the weight of that sadness. He wondered whether Sajit knew more.

"Meanwhile," said the Princeling, "let's watch the dancing moons."

Night had fallen completely. And Tijas knew that it was a special night; when all the moons of Urna could be seen at the same time, and in the same quadrant of the night; when their motions and apparent motions all came together to create the dance, from the hurtling Eríkion to the stately Arráz, the paired Kalíth and Ralíth, the jagged Harikozmá. "And you told me you thought they were singing, too. Singing for you alone, Sajit."

He toyed with Sajit's hair and Tijas felt a twinge of ... some strange emotion ... that

there was something other than ruler and slave that passed between them. But Sajit merely said, "Let me sing now, and it will be as though the moons have been given a voice."

"You shall both sing."

The boys readied their whisperlyres. "Sing to me," said Orifec, "the song that I first heard you sing in the forest; the song that you thought the moons were singing, only you realized it was you yourself."

They sang:

It is not the wind
It is not the moons.
The snow is aflame,
yet the heart has frozen.
I am not I
You are not you.
The song is but motion
in the still air.

And Orifec, thinking, it seemed, of a past that the boys could not imagine, began to weep again. There, alone save for two insignificant children, surrounded by corpses that continued to simulate eating and drinking and laughter as they had been programmed to do.

Finally it seemed he could bear it no longer, and he held up his hand once more for the music to stop.

"I did not think we would meet this way," he said, "and I did not think that it would be this brief."

"My Lord," Tijas said, "what do you mean?"

"Can we comfort you?" Sajit said. "Is that why we're here, to ease your troubled soul?"

"No!" Orifec cried out. "You are here because of my selfishness! My own selfishness! Even you, Doppel-Sajit, know that you have no right to exist, that you are an abomination. But oh, how I wanted to protect Sajit!"

"My Lord," Sajit said, "you never even knew me before."

"No, I never did. I knew nothing, yet I knew everything. Sajit-without-a-Clan, all that you know about yourself is untrue. And I cannot tell you the truth. I cannot. Especially not now. Look up at the sky."

The smudge they had remarked on earlier, in the flight over the city ... it was bigger now, almost eclipsing the moon called Harikozmá. And it was still growing.

"What is it, Starry Highness?" Tijas asked.

Orifec beckoned to the nearest corpse, and it brought him a tray of viewing-crystals. Orifec picked one up and said to Tijas, "Hold it up to your eye." Tijas did.

Magnified, Tijas could see that the smudge was made up of sleek, metallic cylinders, thousands upon thousands, swirling like bacilli in a culture dish. It was less a smudge now; reflecting the moons' light, they were beginning to glisten, like the crystal nematodes that carpeted the chamber.

"People bins," Sajit whispered.

"Two things at once. A culling was planned already; the High Inquest needs its childsoldiers, and every child who fulfills the seven criteria of perfection will be chosen. That is the first thing. That is why I pulled you from the village. That is why I sent the doppling kit. That is why it is so appalling that you, Sajit, couldn't control your curiosity. Do you realize how much more difficult this is, with the two of you having seen each other, touched each other, bonded in a way that is more than brother to brother, more than lover to lover, because you are literally one flesh? And Sajit — you even *named* the unnameable. Opening the box has undone everything. You will never live down the pain."

Sajit said, "It's not about pain. I've got someone now, someone who knows me completely. My whole life I felt that I was living in the wrong world, that my parents were not my family. Now — it's changed." And he gripped Tijas fiercely. Tijas cried out. And Sajit felt his pain.

But in that moment Tijas knew that he and Sajit did not understand the world in the same way.

For Tijas existed for one purpose only; to avoid the culling. When the High Inquest came to take the childsoldiers away, Tijas was destined to go as Sajit. Sajit would remain ... and Tijas, almost certainly, would die ... as almost all childsoldiers died. Those were the words of an ancient song, about a million young boys who dreamed of the stars:

ekáqila eméruat mílilas
nendé z néqilas erdhándat

one hundred thousand became childsoldiers;
ninety-nine thousand died

"You made me so you could kill me," Tijas said.

"In case," said Orifec, "only in case ... otherwise you were not to be quickened."

Sajit said, "Nothing will part us, Starry Highness. I did what was forbidden; I quickened my doppling and came to know him. We feel each other's pain. I think sometimes we even hear each other's thoughts. What will happen if he dies in a war, in another world? Am I going to feel his death on the other side of the galaxy? Will I die too? Never! Tijas is Sajit."

Tijas was moved by his doppling's firmness, but in his heart he knew how it must end.

"There is, in any case, a larger issue now," Orifec said. "Ten sleeps ago, a tachyon bubble came to the city."

The boys gasped. Only the High Inquestors could travel by tachyon bubble, a conveyance that required a star's death to fuel it. "The Inquestor bore a sealed command. He came himself; that was a special honor."

"Urna will *fall beyond!*" Sajit cried.

"No. It is ... an error. The entire Dispersal of Man is linked, through thinkhive upon thinkhive, strands of consciousness reaching through the overcosm, from planetary thinkhives through the hearts of stars, all the way to the great thinkhive that is the soul of Uran s'Varek. It is a very ... *complex* ... construct. Mistakes happen. And this is a very tiny one; a decimal place somewhere, an infinitesimal error ... it seems that Urna is

too insignificant, too backward a world to register on one of their grand indexes. Somewhere on the other side of the Dispersal, a planet *fell beyond* a thousand years ago; its evacuated peoples, in stasis and packed into people bins for a millennium, are now slated to rebuild their world on an empty planet ... which happens to be Urna. Apparently there weren't any people here when that decision was made; and though for us it was a thousand years, for the Inquestors who were playing *makrúgh* with the destinies of worlds, it may only have been a matter of a few moments."

"Then the culling — how can it proceed?" Sajit said. Perhaps this mistake had saved them!

"*Enguéstrens sepáta devénd' áspatut.*" An Inquestor's word may never be unspoken. "That was a different game of *makrúgh*. It is a virtual impossibility that both games should have snared the same world. The culling will be soon. By then, Urna will have been renamed Alykh. Small as it is, our population will not need to be moved to make way. We will merely be swallowed up by another world, another culture."

"And you, Starry Highness?" Sajit said.

"Oh, me. I am deposed. I have a tennight's notice, of course. Ten planetary sleeps to close up the affairs of my royal house. Just as well. We were not a very good ruling family. Cruel, always killing one another for the power, not understanding of course that the power is so fleeting. Many generations ago, the High Inquest raised us up to rule here. I would have been happier ... let us not speak of it. I had a brother, too, once."

A doppling? Tijas thought.

In silence, they gazed up at the sky. The moons did not sing. The cluster of people bins moved closer. Now, with the naked eye, one could make them out. They would be landing soon.

"Go home, boys," said the Princeling of Urna. "And you, Tijas ... get back inside that box. All this has been a dream."

And this was to be marveled at: *he had called Tijas by his name.*

***

"They're not splitting us up," Sajit whispered. "They're not. Not *ever*. I'll never let it happen."

Tijas said listlessly, "But for now ... we'd better go back separately."

So Sajit left the royal chamber by the same displacement plate that Tijas had entered with; Tijas said he would go back by a different route.

When they reached their apartment, Areon sent the girls to bed. They had been stuffed with *peftifesht* and chocolate, and were awake long past their bedtime anyway. Sh

"It's time," Areon said to his son, "for us to talk about the thing we should have talked about before even moving to Shírensang."

"I already know about the doppling kit, father."

"Then you will have guessed that we are on notice; that the High Inquest will soon arrive, and the most suitable children of our world will be given the honor of serving the High Inquest. In all probability of dying for the High Inquest. You are one of the chosen. Naturally; you possess the seven superior qualities they are looking for."

"Yes, father. When the summons comes, we're to open up the kit, and quicken the child inside, send the Doppel-Sajit in for selection. And I will return to my music."

"You sound ... listless. Do you understand that this will save your life? Through the generosity of the Royal Family, you have a chance at a greater destiny?"

Ina said, "Don't badger him. We have to tell him the other thing, too."

"Why?" said his father.

"Because ... we may lose him. Even with that *thing* inside the box."

This is it, Sajit thought. I knew it. They've been keeping something from me all my life ... and now they have to tell me.

"We're not your real parents," Ina said.

Why was it not a surprise?

***

The baby in the hallway, the basket, the token of remembrance ... it was a melodramatic story from a shabby holodrama. Oh, Sajit listened, but it never quite seemed to be real. Although it did explain why all his life he had never felt that he belonged ... *My whole life is a tale told by a street bard for a few coins,* he thought.

Until his mother produced the actual basket, and he gasped — because the basket had been handing from the holosculpt arbor in the simulated forest that walled their living quarters.

"That's no basket!" He had been delivered to his new parents inside the soundbox of a whisperlyre. He had been delivered to this house in a musical instrument, resting on a tangle of snapped lyre-strings. And next above the fretboard there was set an intaglio in lapis, carved with intertwined serpents. *It was a symbol he knew.* And a piece of cloth — not even clingfire, but old-fashioned fabric woven from plants, the old way ... such as the very poor might wear, or the very fashion-conscious. Imprinted with the same insignium. *A sign Sajit recognized. The blue mating serpents. The serpent columns of the throneroom. The serpents in the Princeling's ring.*

Sajit did not really listen after that. It was an overload of revelations. First the world as he knew it coming to an end, then the prospect of losing his other self, of one day being an intimate of the planet's highest power, the next that power being cast down; adding a secret origin story to all this was overkill. He did not care. He tried to listen, but his eyes glazed over as his parents earnestly told the tale of how they had received mysterious e-moluments that enabled them to settle in this village and got his father a secure occupation tending the thinkhive; about how a mysterious woman, cloaked in shadow, had been seen leaving the hallway, a veiled woman.

... a woman Sajit had seen before ...

A woman who really existed!

It was when his parents spoke of the veiled woman that an idea, half-formed, sprang into Sajit's mind. It was rash, but for him it was the only thing left to do. And he was going to have to do it *tonight*.

***

"We're going *now*," Sajit told Tijas. "We're running away."

It was the dead of night, and all but one of the moons had set, the runt moon, alone and visibly spinning. It was a time of night called the Afterdance, after the rare display of all the moons in their intricate patterns, when the people of Urna tended to shutter their dwellings and opaque their windows ... an old superstition from a time when people had not counted the moons nor measured their revolutions, and thought they might never return.

It was the dead of night and the city square was empty. And all they carried was the soundless old whisperlyre, and a single loaf retrieved at the last minute from the larder.

A slow, solemn drumbeat. From across the square there was a slow procession. A line of about a hundred people ... no, servocorpses, for they moved with a precision that proved they were not alive ... the faces of the dead were white in the lone moon's light. Each carried some precious object; a vase, a robe, a holosculpt, a jewel-box.

At the head of the line, not riding a hoverthrone, not carried on a palanquin, wearing only a white robe: the Princeling of Urna.

"Walk with me a while," he said. "I am going to the edge of Nevéqilas." It did not seem an appalling moral outrage that two dopplings were seen together. Of course, they were sur-rounded only by the dead. There was no one to be outraged.

"You're leaving your palace behind?" Sajit said.

"Halát eyáh nishis," said the Princeling. *Everything is nothing.*

"Starry Highness," Tijas said, "do you have no wife, no children?"

"I did, little one. I had them all killed. It was a matter of honor; it pains me still. I wish I had them back, but I had no choice."

No use thinking about the village. No use thinking about the family. Sajit walked on. Presently the line reached a displacement plate and the corpses vanished one by one. Sajit followed Orifec, keeping his thoughts blank so that Orifec's subvocalized command would also cover his own displacement.

The line of corpses emerged on a field on the other side of the Lake of Loons. The cloud of people bins filled half the sky now. They were braking against the atmosphere, each one thrumming in its own frequency. How unlike the cry of the loons when they lit up in synchronized flight! These bins jangled, crashed into one another, moved without regard for the people inside, for the people were all time-frozen, in stasis for who knows how many centuries.

Across the lake, the crystal stamens of Nevéqilas pierced the night sky. And the lone moon drifted.

Then, without warning—

The bins began to fall! From being packed together they broke apart, each seeking its predetermined coordinates. Four bins were swerving, swooping down toward the lake, aiming to land on the field. Each people bin, Sajit saw, could have held a city. The world that had *fallen beyond* must have been far more populous, more urban, than Urna. No wonder they had dismissed the people of Urna from their calculations.

Now came a wind, sweeping down from above, swirling about them. The tall grass whispered. The four bins were settling now. First one, the other three hovering above, a shattering roar first, then a low thrum just at the threshold of hearing; Sajit's very bones shook.

The bin that landed first opened. Then came silver spiders, thousands upon thousands, each as big as a house, scurrying, skittering, planting poles in soil, floating in and out, viewing the world with eyes on stalks ... planting metal pods in the soil that burst asunder and spewed out houses and shops and temples, once collapsed into pellets, now splitting and climbing and spitting out awnings and walkways as though cities were animate cells, splitting, exploding ... "They're growing a city in front of our eyes!"

"And no one to see it but us."

"Why?" Sajit said. "Where are all the citizens of Shirensang? We are a provincial backwater, but a million souls isn't *nobody!*"

"Fear," said the former Princeling. "Something you boys clearly lack. Nothing ever happens on Urna. The world is petrified."

Sajit believed it. They were all cowering in their apartments ... his family ... Arbát ... the chocolate vendors ... the servocorpse mechanics ... but Sajit felt no fear at all. He felt ... wonder. He felt alive. He felt the way a song feels before it is born.

The city, all spirals and spikes and crenellations and mazes and tunnels and turrets, shooting upwards and outwards ... atop it all, a starport ... *This new world is no backwater,* Sajit thought.

And suddenly it was raining people.

The three other people bins began disgorging them! People, frozen people, each wrapped in a skin of stasis. They were within but outside the world. They flew out in flurries, clattered onto the streets of their new city. They were piled up in heaps in the square. The people bins themselves began to come apart as they floated to the surface. The spider robots took each fragment and incorporated it into the city; here a mirror-wall, there a elevated walkway. Smaller spiders rushed about, nailing displacement plates every few meters. Trees sprang up out of nutrient sacs, instantly blossoming. At length the spiders finished their work; their finishing touch was to disassemble each other, until they too vanished into the seams of the city.

"Airang," said Orifec, "the pleasure city, hedonistic capital of a world named A-lykh."

The city stretched all the way to the lake. The humming of machines, the clatter of metal spiders, was silenced. Nothing moved. There were domes. There were columns topped with statues. There were holosculptures in erotic poses, frozen in mid-lovemaking. And piles of people everywhere, frozen, too. Then —

A call from the sky like the blast of a trumpet! The heaps of humans, released instantly from stasis! People sprang to life, stood up, looked about them, dazed for moment, then continuing in mid-action; the city, their surroundings, must have been familiar to them. The silence broke, became a hubbub, a torrent of conversation. *Klazmurah* music, clamorous and plaintive, from congested alley. It was as if the planet Alykh had been taken in an instant, and brought to another world, with no time having elapsed.

And voices everywhere. Laughter. Crude jokes. Chanting from gleaming temples — this then was a religious world, which Urna was not.

For a while the watched, awestruck, then—

"But now," said Orifec, "there is something else that the High Inquest must do. A little bit of ... cutting and polishing. Filing down the rough edges of their handiwork. Look, Sajitteh, look toward the other side of the lake."

That was were the palace of Nevéqilas stood.

Suddenly, above the palace, thousands upon thousands of lights! "Look long and hard! Use the viewing-crystal." A servocorpse came to Sajit with a tray.

He put the crystal to his eye and then he saw what it was. But first he heard it.

Though it was more than a klomet away, the shrill relentless sound of a million children's voices rent the air:

Ishá ha! Ishá ha! Ishá ha ha hé ha! It was the warcry of the childsoldiers. The most feared sound in the universe. The sound of killing innocence.

For every point of light was a child on a spinning hoverdisk. And with each warcry came shafts of laser light, one from each eye, a million children, two million deadly streams of brightness. As one, the army swivelled, swooped, in a complex ballet, and with their laser-eyes they sliced the crystal stamens of the palace, ignited the minarets, carved up the towers — a pyrotechnic display of utter elegance and barbarity.

"My family?" said Sajit. "Are they—"

"In all probability, yes. Though the two games of *makrúgh* where in conflict, each Inquestral command had to be obeyed. I am sure it was carefully worked out, to inflict the minimum amount of damage ... within the precepts of the High Compassion. But your family were part of the royal household; they will have fallen under the prescribed norms of collateral devivement."

"Why?" Sajit cried. And he could find no answers, not in the blank expression of the Princeling who had lost everything, not in Tijas's face either, for though Sajit and Tijas were one in some respects, Tijas had never known Ina and Areon as a family.

He knew he could never be childsoldier. But only a child possessed the reflexes that could control the laser-irises of death. Only a child could learn the utter ruthlessness of an Inquestral war. Only a child could be pitiless, because he did not yet have pity to unlearn.

To be one of *millions,* to be a cog it that relentless machine of death ... *No. I was not born for that.*

"I'll never be one of them. And neither will Tijas."

"They will still plan the culling," Orifec said. "And you will still be on their list ... their very specific list ... you can't escape your DNA."

Sajit looked away from the crumbling city across the lake. He looked at Alykh.

He saw a city just awakening to like. Although he knew that his family might be killed, he felt no emptiness, no pain. It was happening to someone else. *The High Inquest is so vast and uncaring that my whole family, even my city, my world, can fall under "collateral norms" ... so why is my DNA so specific, that they would relentlessly single me out?* It made no sense.

At the edge of the city, there stood a woman. A woman cloaked in shadow....

And the woman looked past Sajit, looked at the Princeling, and she *recognized* him.

"You see her!" Sajit cried. "I'm not just imagining her."

Orifec said, "You must find her. She may have an answer for you." And then he touched Sajit on the cheek and Sajit saw the ring, the intaglio that matched the beat-up whisperlyre's. And Orifec said simply, "Take it." And he pulled the ring from his finger and put it in the boy's palm, and closed the boy's fingers over it. It felt cold and hard.

Sajit said, "Are *you* my father?"

Orifec said, "It would not be seemly to answer that question. But come. No one except the dead can see us. We are no one in this new world. You may as well hug me."

And so Sajit put his arms around the man who had once been an untouchable lord, and they embraced; and in giving freely of himself, Sajit received his own freedom in return. Yet there was no comfort in this.

He broke away. "Come on, Tijas," he said, "We have to find the woman."

But she was already gone.

"Come on, Tijas," he said again.

"Where will we go?"

"I don't know, Tijas. A-way. Away."

He took Tijas's hand and they sprinted across the field, to the walls of a wider world.

Interlude
Elloran

Ton Elloran n'Taanyel Tath had been listening intently to the Rememberer. The more he heard, the less sense the story seemed to make, the less it connected with what he knew to be true.

And yet, through the Rememberer's art, through his art of mimicking voices, of picking the most telling metaphors, of describing the very air that the characters breathed, he came to believe that the Rememberer's words *must* be true. A Rememberer may not lie, after all. It is an impossibility.

And what evidence remained of this fantastical tale, except for the telling of it?

Urna was shattered; Alykh too, having blossomed on this planet for a few centuries, had been hurriedly packed off and was waiting in orbit around elsewhere, to start again, for *there is history, and there is no history; the cosmos must ever eddy, yet be still; such was the central paradox that was Inquestra dogma.*

"Perhaps," said Elloran to his host, who had been Remembering for some days now, barely pausing for a snack, "you can show me the museum. Is there an artifact there, perhaps, something tangible from this other past?"

For the whisperlyre behind the forceshield, the whisperlyre that Elloran recognized as the one Sajit held, now centuries in the past, was not the one in the Rememberer's story. There was no double-serpent intaglio. There was something not right about it.

"Ah, *hokh'Ton*, you will already have noticed that the whisperlyre on display, so venerated, so ancient, is actually a copy," said Tash Teléon.

"It is no more authentic than ... that holosculpt."

He pointed to a doorway that led to an inner courtyard. It was guarded by twin images of Sajit as a child, both woven of light.

"Come, *hokh'Ton*, I will show you where the real artifacts are kept."

***

If the shrine was unswept and rundown, the inner sanctum was chaos. There was a circular displacement plate in the center; that was the only clear space. Around it, up to its very edge, were piles of objects. Musical instruments, old robes, sheafs of music notations, some even scratched by hand on frayed bark-*papél*. There were holoflats and holosculpts.

There was the old wooden bench described by the Rememberer ... the doppling kit. So that part of the story had a tangible object behind it.

To Elloran's astonishment, its controls still lit up when he ran his fingers along the old wood, warm to the touch, as any living, organic matter would be.

The kit still held a charge. For a moment a thought ...

No! He dismissed it. *On Sajit's world, it's an a-bomination.*

Although that world is dead.

***

Tash Toléon spread a piece of cloth over the displacement plate so they would not accidentally be spirited away with an unintended subvocalization.

He fetched a stool for the Inquestor. He clapped his hands and a chilly, bluish light spread out from the walls and ceiling, which was low, claustrophobic.

"The old whisperlyre...."

The Rememberer squeezed easily amongst the old artifacts; of course, as a Rememberer, he kept the location of each one carefully pinpointed in his trained brain; that was his art. He pulled the instrument from under a pile of *papéli*. It was light; the Remember held it by its fingerboard, between two fingers, as he handed it to the Inquestor.

And when Elloran touched it, he felt what he had not felt with the replica. "I wept before," he said. "What I feel now is too deep even for weeping."

But there was no intaglio either.

"I know what you're thinking, *hokh'Ton,*" Tash Toléon said. "But feel the body more closely. There. Where the frets end."

The Inquestor ran his finger again along the wood. Was there a circular depression? Nothing there to see. But did the wood hold some ancient memory of a jewel, long ago pried loose?

"It was removed," he said. "Why?"

"Perhaps we will find out," said Toléon, "as my Remembrance proceeds."

Then Elloran said, "But, the Princeling, Orifec ... was he Sajit's real father? For what I have always believed was that his father was a nameless *dorezda* who visited the stews of Alykh."

"A man can have many fathers," Toléon said.

"But only one mother," Elloran said, "for we can see who gave him birth. Unless the womb was a doppling kit."

Elloran spotted a holoflat of a woman. He pulled it from another heap of *papéli*.

He recognized her immediately because of Tash Toléon's powerful Remembering. And he could see, though shadow swirled about the image, that the woman's eyes were the eyes of Shen Sajit. "The woman cloaked in shadow," he said.

"Yes."

"And who *is* the woman cloaked in shadow?"

"Ah, the woman. I must speak of her next. So my story, as a pebble in a pond, must ripple outward, wider, stepping earlier in the past that we may reach out later into the future...."

to be continued....

NEXT ISSUE
BOOK TWO:
A WOMAN CLOAKED IN
SHADOW

Professor Schnau-en-Jip

Frequently Asked Questions about the Inquestral Highspeech

What kind of language is the Inquestral Highspeech?

Bhasháhokh, the Inquestral Highspeech, is a ceremonial, poetic, and somewhat potent language in that its words are considered to be entities in themselves, imbued with a quasi-magical reality. The roots of the language are clearly Indo-European, meaning that it is the only classical language of the Dispersal of Man that claims any kind of link with Old Earth (known as the Homeworld of the Heart amongst Inquestral poets.) However, there is no known Indo-European language that can be seen as its direct antecedent, so it must be seen as its own subfamily. There are similarities to Latin, Greek, and Sanskrit, but nothing that would render the language mutually intelligible with any ancient Earth language.

However, the work of Professor Jan Murphy has shown that, using basic Indo-European linguistics, most structures in the language can be relatively easily analysed.

During the period of the Dispersal of Man, *Basháhokh* is not exactly a commonly spoken language. Its elaborate rules and complex inflections are learned only by Inquestors and those who live and work in their sphere of influence, while others speak various forms of lowspeech, some of which are clearly descended from Inquestral, others not.

In the time of Sajit, noun declensions, once very specific to each noun class, have become rather uncommon in normal speech, and in poetry the creator is able to choose, within reason, from many sets of obsolete and obsolescent inflections. We will find, often within the same poem, or even the same line, alternate forms, often used deliberately for poetic effect. Apart from the eight cases that are found in early Indo-European languages, *Bhasháhokh* also has an *intensive case* which is used when two nouns in apposition would normally be in the same case. This is a frequent poetic usage and also an aid in scansion.

Here is a schema of all the possible endings in the Highspeech noun paradigm. In earlier times, endings were specific to certain noun classes (declensions) and there were many exceptions. Gender was also an important factor, but the various genders and possible endings started to be used interchangeably as the Highspeech became essentially a "historic" language, a language only used in poetry and in elevated speech. Many gender-specific forms merged. During the high classic era in which Sajit and other lyric poets lived, this schema was considered the standard paradigm, though numerous other forms can be found throughout the literature.

dáve, stem *dávek-*, a boy.

	Singular	Dual	Plural
Nominative	{dáve }	{dávey }	{dávek•(e)r, •ai}
Vocative	{davéh}	{daveýh }	{dávek•es, •as}

Accusative	dávek•eh, •en	{dáveyh }	{or irreg. }
Genitive	dávek•s, •i, •ens	dávekys	dávk•yh, •ah,•ã, •s
Dative	dávek•en, •in	dávekyn	davék•an, •aran
Ablative	davéki		davéky	dávek•ai, •ei,
(•an)			
Intensive	{ davek•n, y'davék•oten, y'dávek•n }		
Locative	daveká	daveký	davékein
Temporative	davek•aín	davek•ýn	davekeín

Notes:

The intensive "case" is not really a case per se but an intensifier.   If two closely associated nouns appear together, the actual case ending is attached to the first while the second may appear with an intensive ending instead of a case ending.

The accusative case is distinctive only in the singular, as Nom., Voc., and Acc., have merged in the dual and plural with forms being interchangeable.

Though it is possible to discern a basic SVO word order in High Inquestral, the reality is that since virtually all surviving texts are poetic, SVO is statistically only slightly more common than other orders. It is only because of the differentiation of the accusative singular case that the slight prevalence of the SVO structure can be distinguished.

The Pronunciation of the Highspeech

In a sense, this is a purely academic question because no native speakers have been discovered at this time of publication.   There were several dialects, but in the

Inquestor novels, the standard is usually considered to be the dialect of Varezhdur.

In subsequent issues (once the creation of Inquestral font can be completed) there will be more detailed discussion using the actual script. However, we can probably give a few basic guidelines for the time being:

The following vowels are distinguished in official grammars of *bhashahokh,* in the standard transliteration

a similar to Italian.

e varies between the closed and open *e* sound in Italian.

i a closed sound.

o generally an open sound.

u a pure, rounded sound, as it boot.

y in Inquestral, this sound represents the vowel ʉ in IPA

yu this diglyph is used to represent a sound similar to German ü.

All seven vowels may be long or short, though long vowels are quite rare in standard Inquestral. All seven vowels may be nasalized. Nasalization is represented in Inquestral script by a subscript n, and in the transliteration by a following *h* or by a tilde (a weaker nasalization.)

Most consonants are pronounced as in English, except that:

The letters *p, t,* and *k* are not aspirated. To represent the aspirated series, an h is added in transliteration. *Kh* tends towards the sound of *ch* in *loch.* *C* represents the unaspirated version of English *ch* as in *church*, so it is a sound similar to the *tj* in Dutch *beetje*. The letter *q* represents in some dialects a very strongly aspirated *c* sound, but in others a sound more similar to the *ch* of German *ich*.

Every word in *bhashahokh* except enclitics has a tonic accent which in careful writing is represented by an acute accent. The accent has to be learned, because it is often unpredictable. In nouns, the accent may shift in the course of declension.

Pronouns

Personal pronouns are optional in *bhashahokh* and technically are not used in the third person. Instead, in the third person, a demonstrative may be used. The demonstrative pronoun system is extremely complex, allowing for four degrees of propinquity and three degrees of hierarchy: exalted, high and humble, and are declined for all three numbers and all cases except the vocative.

In the first and second persons different pronouns are used according to the relative status of the conversationalists.

	I	YOU
high-high	ísh	dú, dó
high-humble	ísh	tú, téi
humble-high	sarnáng	hokhté
humble-exalted	sarnáng	zyh
exalted-humble	ísh	yng

In addition to the demonstratives, the following are sometimes found in a third person pronominal function

neutral/inanimate	úton, éng
high/animate	hokhté
exalted/animate	zyh

These language notes will be continued in the next issue of *Inquestor Tales*.

Trilogies, Ursine Predators, and Tree-Rich Areas

by Markus Thierstein

I recently spent a few days in Berlin.

Now, this is not something very unusual in itself, and you might be wondering why I feel compelled to mention this. It's simple. You might be aware of the accepted wisdom that the book (and records, films et al) that affect you the most, that leave the deepest impression and shape your view of the world forever are the ones you encounter as impressionable pre/teenagers.

But when, during said trip to Berlin, I encountered a poster advertising a concert by a band called Black Rainbow was instantly taken back to a book I had read in my 40s which had left a huge and lasting impression; back to a world, nah, a universe of over-stylised honour, of dealy games being played with humanity, and of artists' ways of dealing with and reacting to these games.

And to the Darkweaver Ir Jenjen's Black Rainbow from The Darkling Wind, the final instalment in Somtow Sucharitkul's Inquestor Trilogy.

Now, I presume you are familiar with said trilogy in 4 books (the author clearly has been taking notes from Douglas Adams' approach to trilogies) - epic in scope, poetic in execution and tone; essentially large, sweeping Space Opera which could just as well have been High Fantasy in it its conception if it wasn't for the SFnal trappings.

What most attracted me to these stories was the overall poetical language, the stories interspersed with songs and poetry in several languages and scripts, the philosophical and emotional scope in the stories, ambiguous as it is; and the remarkable elegance and constraint shown by the author whilst dealing with topics and story lines which could have ended up saccharine and/or overblown in lesser hands.

But what really startled me, with every book I picked up, were the horrendous, sickly faux-fantasy covers that graced them. Horrifying, misleading, and something to marvel at in disbelief. (the re-release in 2013 was better, or at least more conventional, by a long way, I have to admit)

The Inquestors of the stories, their lives, motives, motivations remain tantalizingly ever so slightly out of the grasp of the reader I found. But we are clearly shown the black hole at the heart of the Inquest, infusing it with a grand, profound, and all-suffusing sadness, as well as a cynicism (the author's?) which keeps coming through in the stories. And both of these mirror our lives, our world, even without a mysterious Inquest in the centre to hold it all together.

There is no history, and history there is.

These are the opening words of the game of Makrugh, played by Inquestors playing for honour, power, and the end of planets, civilisations, people. Which in turns leads to a surprising amount of death, destruction, horrors for books with such and artistic and poetic slant.

But now, every time I misspell my name when signing an email message, I am reminded of the musician Sajit, one of the key personas in the larger story arc, and of the fact that Somtow Sucharitkul is writing a 5th novel for the series centring on Sajit (see above for a comment on 'trilogies').

But is a new Inquestor novel a big deal? Well, if you ask me, I would have to tell you that we are in ursine predator/tree-rich area territory. Or to put is simpler - I'm ridiculously excited about it, and so should you be, too!

Original magazine cover from 1981, cover by George Barr, for *The Rainbow King*

The Rainbow King

Original lead-in from Isaac Asimov's Science Fiction Magazine:

Mr. Sucharitkul assures us that there is an Inquestor book in the making. Meanwhile, here is an Adventure ...

No use thinking of glory. No use thinking of distant starships that seemed to stand still against the starlight. No use thinking of a girl's charred body, gift-wrapped in ribbons of warped steel.

Sajit turned his back on the fire and shook off the memories. There wasn't any time. The flames were gaining on him, hissing down the corridors of the doomed starship.

He ran.

His fursoles pattered on the mirror metal, the only sound save the fire's whisper in this worm's gullet of a corridor that twisted away from the ship's heart, bypassing the weaponry levels and the living levels and the observing levels. It wasn't meant for people— only for maintenance equipment. Ahead, in the curve of the wall, reflections of the fire behind him danced. He'd found the corridor his first day aboard the ship. He hadn't told anyone. Sajit was a survivor.

He had grown up fleecing the *dorezdas* in the jungle-streets of Aírang on his homeworld, and he'd fought his way through two terrible wars.

I can't die now! he was thinking. I've already been through too much! He was twelve years old.

He flung his cloak behind him, sacrificing it to the fire. *That'll slow you down!* He threw out all his weapons, until he was down to the bundle he had packed away in case it ever came to this. If it would only stop to consume the cloak and the weapons and not catch up with him—

And there was the hatch he wanted. He shoved at it with his whole body—he had not much weight to put into it—but it wouldn't give. It was too cramped to make a dash and crash it open, and he felt the heat behind him, he felt his blood ready to boil and the sweat streaming—

An idea. He turned his laser-irises on the doorway and sizzled the metal with a lethal stare, then wriggled through a stomach-wrenching gravity reversal—

And landed lightly on his feet. He was where he hoped he'd be: the launch hangar of the Inquestors. A wide ledge that extended outside the d e l p h i n o i d   s t a r s h i p, protected from empty space by an insubstantial dome of force. Above, the stars shone.

Straight ahead, so far that they looked like toys, three dead ships floated, three silver amulets hanging in the blackness. When he craned his neck he could see how the upper levels of his own ship had been pried open and shredded by the attackers. Whoever they had been. It had been one side or the other, waiting in ambush at the transdimensional nexus as they burst blind out of the overcosm into realspace. It didn't matter who it had been. The Inquestral mission had failed.

And here on the hangar, just as Sajit had hoped, shiny-new and sleek as a wild silverdove, was the Inquestral landing craft.

If things had gone as they should have, this lander would have come to Ymvyrsh and the Inquestors would have stood in the parched fields of the razed planet, tall, their shimmercloaks blushing in the wind, their faces serene, old, unruffled as they dictated the terms of the Inquestral peace upon the warring worlds of Ymvyrsh and Ainverell. Sajit could see the scene now: the Inquestors standing, calm and compassionate, while husks of old buildings fell burning to the ground ... it was not to be. No Inquestor would come to Ymvyrsh now. Only a young boy who wanted to be alive.

He clutched his bundle under his arm. It seemed thinner than before, and something metal was digging into his side, cold. The starlight, unseen for the three subjective months of overcosm travel, was strange to him; here too there was coldness. He moved quickly to the landing craft, shivering. He didn't want to admit the cold was fear.

He found the entrance and opened it, sliding his slight body easily down the shaft. There were two rooms, like pears joined at the stems: the one he was in was wide enough for two or three adults. Half-light, bluish and diffuse, played over shelves of provisions. That was good —he'd have to learn to operate the lander somehow, he'd have to find Ymvyrsh— he'd need food.

I'll find Ymvyrsh somehow. A world's a world, even when it's at war, he thought fiercely. I'll sing for a few cheap meals, or if they're too poor I'll find something less honorable to do....

He crept towards the passageway that led to the control room. If the lander was at all like a standard short-range vessel, there would be no problem, but—

The lander lurched to life! Sajit was jerked forward into the control cabin. He felt violent pain in his foot and wondered distantly whether it was broken. For a moment he closed his eyes. The lander had been on automatic! His plans were ruined!

When he opened his eyes he saw a swath of blue fur that rippled, the hem of a robe that shimmered pink against the dark blue....

"Lord Inquestor!" he whispered, knowing he must be in the presence of one of the rulers of the Dispersal of Man. He did not dare look up. When he tried to move his foot, pain stabbed him. He had to say something. "I am Sajit-without-a-clan, born on the world Alykh and three years a soldier of the Inquest," he said, keeping his eyes fixed on the hem of the shimmercloak. The shimmercloak sparkled, a million jewel facets in the living cloth. He was almost hypnotized by it.

The Inquestor said nothing for a long time. When he spoke, it was not the authoritative voice of an old man. It was a young voice, a voice that struggled to master terror. "I am," the Inquestor said, "Ton Elloran n'Taanyel Tath, Inquestor-that-is-to-be."

Sajit looked up. Above the sparkling raiment was the face of a boy, perhaps only a year or two older than Sajit himself. "You're only a —" he burst out, then bit his tongue.

"Yes, a boy," Ton Elloran said. "Get up, Sajit-without-a-clan."

"I've hurt my foot."

The other boy knelt down beside him and half-lifted him so that he was leaning against the wall of the passageway. Sajit saw into his eyes, then; but he could not understand what he saw. They were clear, gray eyes that seemed to mask a" terrible loneliness. For a while

they did not speak; and the lander sped on, steadying itself, knowing its destination.

Elloran said, "I have to finish the mission, you know."

"What do you mean, Inquestor, why?"

"When we saw that the ship was doomed, the Inquestors in command chose me, the youngest, to survive. "They decided they had lived long enough...."

"And you will do what four Inquestral ships couldn't do?" said Sajit, dismayed.

"Listen. We tried to send Inquestors to Ymvyrsh a long time ago, by tachyon bubble. We knew from disturbances in the lines of communication, from planetary thinkhive to planetary thinkhive, we knew of this war that has exceeded all proportions the Inquest laid down for such interplanetary wars ... the tachyon bubble systems would not work. The planets had been sealed off to the Inquest; the receiving stations tampered with, refusing all the incoming routes! Can you understand what this means? They have rejected the Inquest, perhaps ... now I must land on Ymvyrsh. I, an Inquestor, inviolate, must find the Inquestor who rules on Ymvyrsh, if he still exists, make arrangements for the war to end, and return to Uran s'VareK. Surely the Inquestor-in-power will have access to a tachyon bubble system — and surely it must work for departures if not for unwanted visitors...."

Sajit saw that he was speaking like a textbook. Didn't the boy know how impossible it would be? Didn't he know that you don't just go charging down to a war-torn planet and make peace?

The boy went on. "I know what you're thinking!" he said, sounding very young suddenly. "You think you should stop me or something. You think I can't do this. You didn't exactly have this in mind when you sneaked aboard this lander instead of dying with the ship as was your duty."

"I didn't come this far to die."

"Why don't you kill me, then? Then you wouldn't be troubled by a meddlesome apprentice Inquestor—"

"Ton Elloran, I didn't say anything about killing—"

"Listen. You are a soldier child of the Inquest, aren't you? You have laser-irises, implanted at the time of your induction, and you could kill me at any time with a glance and a subvocalized command. The ship is yours for the taking."

Sajit looked at the older boy, and he knew he couldn't kill him. You just couldn't kill an Inquestor. It went against everything—

"I told you, Sajit-without-a-clan. To harm me would be to harm yourself. Even a rebel like you can't resist a truth so deeply ingrained. I can perform the Inquest's mission on Ymvyrsh...." Elloran looked away, then got up and clapped his hands, blanking the metal walls-hields to let in the starlight. It must be at least a day's journey to the star Darronderrik around which Ymvyrsh and Ainverell revolved, twin worlds locked in a slow pavane around the same star, in one orbit ... yet never at peace. Sajit could make nothing of the star-stream; he was not one of those to whom the night sky sang. He liked cities. Blackness and stars meant bleakness and war to him....

His foot still ached. He struggled to get up, propped himself against the wall of the linking corridor, and thought: *So much for my clever plans.*

He clenched back a tear. When he saw that Ton Elloran was not looking, he let that tear trickle down, tickling his cheek. Then he tried to stand up and winced with pain, and the bundle he'd wedged under his arm slipped and clattered to the floor, spilling its contents—

Elloran turned, startled.

... Untuned strings jangling ... a sussurant sigh ... a silvery breathy keening ... glint of metal and polished wood and intagliate agates....

Sajit said, half to himself, "At least I haven't lost everything from my past, then."

He picked it up—the whisperlyre—the only thing that linked him to his homeworld and to his nameless father—and cradled it in his arms. Sounds, random, an almost-harmony, cascaded; but he did not play.

For no song came.

***

The two of them travelled on for two or three sleeps, not speaking much, distrusting one another. Through the crystalline shipwalls shone unrecognized stars; and the star Darronderrik grew from pinpoint to topaz cabochon, fireball-brilliant. Sajit slept mostly. But dreams of the past haunted him, and to sleep was as restive as to stay awake....

... Airang, a city of mazes within mazes, chief city of the pleasure- world Alykh, where tall spires stung the violet sky, where the tired and the rootless and the jaded came and bought love and release, and where they rode the varigrav coasters until they had purged all their pain, where they came for a sleep or two and were wooed by the splendor and awed by the glitter and did not see the hovels of those who called the world their homeworld; that was Alykh. A tapestry stitched with jewels and seamed with sewers....

... hurt old eyes that could not quite meet his own, old eyes in a fresh new face, the eternal fresh face of the Alykhish pleasure girl, sung of in a thousand songs, perfect face unlined by worry, face replaced each summer for the new season before the blemishes could come ... the voice: *Leave, Sajit! Leave before I don't have the heart to kick you out. Take the whisperlyre. Take anything you want. I don't want anything left here to remind me of the* dorezda *who spawned you in my womb* ... tall figure of a man waiting. A new *dorezda*.

... growing up in a small room with moulting walls; the displacement plate at the street comer was defunct and overgrown with weeds and you had to walk the four klomets to the streets of the strutting starmen....

... and the whisperlyre. There was a metal-wood harpframe that supported the seven strings for plucking and the sixty-eight sympathetic strings; and in the body of the frame were the thousands of tiny whisper-passages where the ionized wind rushed and reechoed and transmuted the ping of the string into lonely mountains' wuthering and surf-shatter of abandoned shores, the wind that gave the whisperlyre its name, that drew its energy from the heat of your body, so that when you threw all your passion and all your heart into the song you would become cold, like a statue, like a corpse....

... *please sir, take me with you, you're a singer like my father. I'm an orphan sir, help* ...

... beaten and abandoned amid the firesnows of Ont ...

... voice of the tall Inquestor, grip of the restraint-field—Don't run any more, boy. It's over. You'll go to the wars like every other child, and if you return you'll be initiated into a profession and perhaps your singing will stand you in good stead and you'll find a good musicians' clan even . ...

... fingertingle of a taut string, shimmerfade of an afterwhisper, a dying strain, fading, fading ...

***

Sajit woke, clutching his whisperlyre. He wrapped his arms around it, recharging it, feeling the warmth steal away from his body. He was about to play—

—"Come quickly!" the voice of Ton Elloran from the other room.

Sajit limped through the pas-sageway. A planet shone in the darkness, blue-green wisp-streaked with white.

"... Ymvyrsh?"

"You don't understand. Ainverell, Ainverell—it's gone!"

"What do you mean?"

"There's only one planet here when there should be two!"

Sajit went up to the other boy. He touched the edge of an untouchable loneliness and shied away. Elloran said, "It is the right place. The lander doesn't make mis-takes. Ainverell has been obliterated."

"Then the war is over," said Sajit, trying to sound encouraging.

"The background radiation level is low. Ainverell was destroyed a long time ago. Perhaps even a century." Suddenly, Elloran seemed a child, crying for sympathy: "What shall I do now?"

But before Sajit could comfort him he had remembered his place. He had drawn himself up tall, the way Sajit supposed an Inquestor must always be. Sajit said, "Is there nothing in your training to cover this?"

"I'm only an Inquestor-to-he," said Elloran. "Ton Alk-amathdes, my old teacher, would have known. He was half a millennium old or more, and a master utopia hunter...."

"What's a utopia hunter?"

"One who exposes the flaws in utopias, who compassionately brings change and vitality to worlds that think they have found perfection," said Elloran. He seem-ed to be reciting.

"It sounds wrong."

"What would you know, Sajit-without-a-clan?" Elloran turned to watch the planet, which was growing little hy little in the blackness. Then, almost to himself, he said, "Alkamathdes was assigned to rule over Ymvyrsh just before I left on this expedition ... but surely he is Kingling here no longer. We were six subjective months on this journey; in realtime, a century has passed ... he has long moved on to other things, I think."

They stood in silence for some moments, while the planet loomed nearer....

"Ton Elloran," said Sajit, "if Ainverell has been dead for so long, why were we attacked? Who was it who attacked us?"

"I don't know!" Elloran shouted. "What do you think I am, the galactic thinkhive on Uran s'Varek with all the answers? Listen, soldier boy. We're going down on the planet. We're going to find the people in power, locate the Inquestral tachyon bubble system so that I can return to Uran s'Varek and report on the mission—"

"And what about me? You Inquestors can take your tachyon bubbles and flick across the Dispersal of Man in an attosecond. I have to take my chances with time dilation—"

Elloran said, "The Inquest is compassionate. I will take care of you."

"You can't even take care of yourself!" Sajit said hotly. "You're going to land us conspicuously in the middle of enemies and you're going to get us all killed!"

"What is a life to the Inquest?" said Elloran, but his voice quavered. Sajit thought he saw tears, and he was appalled, that an Inquestor should show uncertainty. He turned his back on Elloran and returned to the other chamber.

Later he tried to play the whisperlyre, but could not find more than a few notes. He came out to watch the stars, and to watch Elloran as he stood motionless in the control room. The planet was much nearer now; it filled half the sky. Sajit found no comfort in the thought of earth under his feet. For him every planetfall had always been a scramble to survive....

If it were just me, he thought, I'd make it, somehow. But with him here, not knowing the first thing about survival—

And then he remembered that he had thought he had seen tears in the Inquestor's eyes, and he thought, If an Inquestor can weep, anything can happen. The speed of light can change. We could find a utopia down there.

Ton Elloran n'Taanyel Tath clapped his hands three times, opaquing the ship-walls, putting a shield of mirror metal between them and the threatening planet.

***

The lander circled the planet, trying to find the cities. There should have been cities, certainly; when Elloran summoned up holo-images from the lander's memory, they saw cities with resounding names: Tomistris, Dieker, Zhimward, d'Aihvad, Ang z'Darronderrik, city of the sun, the capital city Undebarang, where floating avenues radiated from a hill-high obelisk carved from a flawless amethyst that had been grown in the Crys-tallizing Sea on Uran s'Varek itself ... they were all gone, these cities, gone without trace.

The lander's orbit spir-alled nearer; they burst through the cloudveil of Ymvyrsh and flew over the land. There were fields that checkered the plains with brown and yellow squares. There were villages, all clustered along narrow roads. Here and there were jade meadows or a crystal serpent of a stream....

The scenery did not change, from one end of the one major land mass to the other. Where Undebarang should have been there was only more of the pastoral landscape. It stretched to the foothills of a mountain range, mist-blue in the distance. And the sky—

Once before had Sajit heard of a sky this blue, and that was in a song about old Earth, before the Dispersal of Man. It was blue and jewel-clear and pure as a ringing octave.

"Do you think—?" he whispered.

"No," Elloran replied coldly. "Earth was never like in the songs. You should know better than that. But no doubt about it ... this world is suspicious. It's the same from shore to shore, and no culture is really like that. It feels ... set up."

"But beautiful."

"I fear it," Elloran said. And then he stopped himself short, and Sajit could tell he was angry at himself for having let down his guard in front of a mere clanless soldier child....

The Inquestor chose a field that lay about where the center of Undebarang should have been, about half a klomet from a cluster of village huts that bordered a winding lane. Softly the lander came down, and they stepped down from the craft.... Sajit found the gravity quite light; he hardly had to limp at all.

He took a few steps out in the bouncy-soft grass, turned, faced the wall of mist-high mountains, and caught his breath. He saw the rainbows.

They arched out from a point somewhere behind the highest peak, resolving from the mists like cadences of a song; they transsected the sky, radiating from a single, hidden, cloud-high point ... they were frozen songs. Chords woven from singing strands of meadow, ruby, tangerine, sky, lapis, topaz, plum; peacock-painted bridges, jewel-candy-arcing, heart-stoppingly still.

Sajit felt very happy. He turned to Ton Elloran, smiling, but he saw no responsive smile. "It's so beautiful!" he cried out.

"Too beautiful." said Elloran curtly. "Let's go into the village now."

"What about provisions?"

"I am an Inquestor. They will provide."

Dismay flooded Sajit. "What do you mean, Ton Elloran? Are you mad or something? Here we are on a strange planet with a lander stuffed with food and we're going to walk into an alien village without anything to eat?"

"I know what I'm doing!" Elloran had begun walking resolutely down a twisty-curving path half-buried in the tall grass, his shimmercloak flapping and making sparks on the emerald green....

"Powers of powers!" Sajit cried. "Don't you care about your own skin, Inquestor?" Just like a damned *dorezda*, thinking he's so important, wouldn't last five minutes on Aírang. He climbed back into the lander, found the provisions shelves, scooped out a couple of handfuls of concentrate packages, found his old bundle on the floor and stuffed it with them. He looked around furtively—street children's habits died hard—and the closeness of the lander's interior oppressed him after the outside. It was then that he realized that Ymvyrsh was a very beautiful world. And comforting, thought the boy, hefting the weight onto his shoulder and making for the exit.

As he left he glanced at the unplayed whisperlyre, abandoned on the mirror metal floor. It was like a recurring dream.

Half-reluctant, he picked it up. The warmth fled from his fingers....

He ran out into the sunshine. Even the whisperlyre felt less cold.

He turned to gasp at the rainbows criss-crossing the blue distance, and then hurried after Ton Elloran ... and caught up with him, breathless. . , .

"I see you wish to throw in your lot with me," said Elloran, looking straight ahead. "That would be wiser."

"No, but I can't just leave you to walk into a—"

Ton Elloran cut him short with a look. They walked on. Presently they came to another field with children at play, pre-warrior-aged, six or seven years old. They were running like wild animals; there was shrill laughter in the sunlight. Sajit saw that they never frowned at all. Sajit felt as though a song were about to burst from him, as he had often felt when he was first learning the old songs, a warmth welling up inside. But he only said, "The war is over." It was a strange thought.

They were approaching the cluster of houses. A few peasants walked by, glancing only cursorily at the two of them; again Sajit saw that they were always smiling—a little vacuously perhaps—in the manner of people who are not used to being stingy with their laughter....

Sajit remembered the streets of his homeworld and was envious.

Elloran was becoming more and more impatient. Finally he went up to a man and stopped him. His blue eyes, gleaming in a wizened face crowned with white wreathlike hair, exuded kindness. He smelled of old earth: pungent, heady, warm.

Elloran said, formally, "I am Ton Elloran nTaanyel Tath, son of Prince Taanyel, Inquestor-who-is-to-be. I am here to seek the Inquestors-that-rule, to end the war between Ymvjrrsh and Ainverell ..."—His voice broke a

little.—"and to bring you peace. Will you give me hospitality and information?"

The old man looked at both of them amusedly and said, finally, "My house is yours, of course. We don't see many strangers here; don't rightly know what an 'Inquestor' may be, but you seem important-looking enough. Be no war here, though. We and the next village are at peace a hundred years, more than that."

Maybe he's right, Sajit thought. Maybe he can automatically get us food because he looks important —or something. But he clutched his parcel tighter, even though reason told him that this wasn't Aírang.

But Elloran seemed annoyed. He was talking to the peasant as though he were an imbecile: "Then who rules here, if you don't know what an Inquestor is?"

The man said (without ever losing his jovial countenance), "Rainbow King rules here, of course. Lookit, over the mountain tops."

Sajit stole a glance at the distant mountains behind

him, with the color-arcs poised above the mistveils....

"Yes," the old man went on, "Rainbow King. Come now, guests, and eat. Journey from next village made you weary. I'm sure."

"Wait!" Elloran shouted after the man, who had already begun to stride towards one of the squat huts. "Who is the Rainbow King? Is he an Inquestor?" But the man was out of earshot.

Sajit said, "It's a beautiful world. Why ask questions, Elloran?"

"You stupid soldier child," Elloran said impatiently. His anger seemed so out of place here. "If this is really the way things are, why were we attacked? Who's trying to fool whom? What would Ton Alkamathdes have done? I wish I had his guidance—"

The warmth of this world stirred in Sajit again. He remembered the smiles everywhere, the jewel-glitter of rainbows, the laughter .. . he wanted to embrace the world. He wanted to forget Alykh and Ont and a dozen stinking worlds and the endless overcosm wars.

"I don't care," he said hotly, "what you say! I only know what I see, and it's—it's a utopia!"

"That's just what I'm afraid of," said the boy Inquestor, and Sajit had never seen anyone look so worn with grief.

***

Sajit liked the house at once—it was so different from the one on Aírang, the peeling, dust-thick house with the painful memories. "This one had four detached L-shaped structures surrounding a central atrium, plain whitewashed walls immaculately clean, leaning roofs neatly thatched, and the air faintly citrus-fragrant. They were shown to their room—one of the four structures—wide windows overlooking a dale where primitive autoploughs moved ponderously, working the land . , . then they went into the atrium, and sat on the furry floor which curved to support the contours of their bodies.

"Forgive me," the old man said, "if my family and I do

not eat with you. We have already eaten, of course."

The family had gathered: a wife and two husbands, two children, drably dressed but brightly smiling; they seemed normal, dignified. The children rushed out to play, the wife and husbands left, and the old man departed after a moment and reentered with food: a tray of fresh shorreth cheese, baked yunaki with the plumage still showing in a vivid blue ring around the drumsticks....

"You see," Elloran said, "wherever one goes, they still cannot deny food to an Inquestor." Sajit began to feel foolish for having dragged the concentrate packages along. The world of the Inquestors was clearly not the world of the streets.

Sajit looked at the old man, whose benign expression seemed unchanged, and said, "And where is it that your Rainbow King dwells?" He thought it must be some kind of folk belief.

"In the mountains. Far. Where all the rainbows meet, stranger. Dangerous, you can't go there—be ptera-

tygers in the mountain peaks...."

"Oh, come on, there are no pteratygers on this planet. Only on Uran s'Varek—" Elloran stopped short. He seemed to be thinking, very hard. Then, abruptly, "Do you never stop smiling, powers of powers?"

"Why should we? Everyone's happy here."

Sajit laughed. "Why shouldn't this planet be a utopia. Ton Elloran?" He reached for a yunaki drumstick—

The old man seized the tray; without another word he left the atrium and entered one of the L-shaped rooms. "What's this?" Sajit cried angrily. "What have we done to make you take away the food?"

There was no answer. Darkness was falling, a little at a time; through one of the four passages out of the atrium they could see the rainbows still, vivid in the graying sky. Sajit saw that Elloran had become very pale; something was in him that Sajit could not touch.

The air chilled a little. He was hungry.

"Well, you should at least thank me for having the presence of mind to bring these." He shook out the bundle. Elloran's hand shot out and grabbed one of the packets. I've been selfish, thought Sajit. This boy's been starving and he's too proud or too preoccupied to say a word. And now he saw the rainbows stained with the crimson of the twilight, and he wondered what kept them in place. Surely they were not natural....

Elloran said, "They don't eat. But they have food, and they pretend."

"Let's go to the room now." Sajit got up; tiredness weighed him down for the first time, and he felt the limp a little. He bundled together the packets and the whisperlyre—they had e-nough food for a couple of days, if they didn't gorge themselves. They turned to go into the guestroom—

"Look!" Sajit heard Elloran's urgent whisper. "Look, through the entry opposite the mountains ... do you remember the auto-ploughs, digging up the field in the valley down there?"

Sajit nodded. They crept up to the entry and stood there a moment. A moon had arisen, hauntingly like the old descriptions of the moons of old Earth, and the fields were eerie black, flecked with mirror metal. ...

"Look carefully!" said Elloran. "Do you see it?"

Sajit strained. He saw the autoploughs move into a pool of moonlight. They were not ploughing now. They were going back, smoothing out the earth, patting it down, restoring it ... Sajit could tell that by morning there would have been no progress. It was all an illusion. Chill claws of fear clutched him. "What'll we do?" he cried, too loud, stifling himself too late.

"We wake them up. We get answers. We find out who is doing this—

"But—"

Elloran had already stalked toward the L-shaped structure into which they had seen the stranger go before. He banged the door-stud with his fist. It shot open—

"Wake up, in the Inquest's name!" he shouted. His voice sounded shrill and small in the huge silence. Moonlight fell into the room.

Blocking the broad stripe of light was the peasant, his face a silhouette. "What's the meaning of these illusions?" Elloran screamed at him. "Who are you trying to delude? Why was this world made to look like a utopia? Why did you destroy the Inquestral mission ship? Who is the ruler of this planet?"

The old man didn't answer. He seemed frozen in place.

Sajit looked deep into his eyes and saw only mirror-blankness. A light wind from the open window played with the old man's hair, but the face never quivered.... Sajit shrank back and found himself backing into the woman. She didn't move. The whole family was gathered in this room like disused dolls on a shelf....

Sajit shivered. He had never feared the *dorezdas* with their brash talk and their gullibility, or being abandoned on strange inhospitable planets, or warships streaking through the overcosm ... he turned to Elloran. "What'll we do?"

Elloran said, "I must complete my mission."

Sajit followed him out of the room and into the atrium; away from the room and the strangely still family he could breathe a little easier. Elloran flicked his head toward the mountains, now a black wall blocking the starlight and buttressed by the rainbows, drained of their jewel colors now, ghost-bridges arcing in the dark....

"We can't go there!" Sajit said. "That's probably the most dangerous place on this planet. After what we've seen I'm ready to believe there are pteratygers in the mountains —"

"Aren't you interested in knowing how millions of people, hundreds of cities, have vanished without a trace?" said Elloran. "I know I don't have to bring peace to this world anymore. It is utterly at peace—it can't be an anything else, since everything is returned to its starting point every morning. But now"—and Sajit was startled by the boy's intensity —"I must hunt down this utopia, Sajit-without-a-clan. Ton Alkamathdes told me that man must dream of utopias always—but to imagine that one has achieved that goal ... is to deny life. The Inquest is built upon this one axiom, Sajit. The quest for the eternal dream, the quest and the never finding, are the heart of the Dispersal of Man...." His eyes were closed and he seemed to be quoting.

"Well," said Sajit, "let's find the lander then."

"We can get some food from there, enough for the journey."

"They had begun walking now, and the house was a hundred meters or so behind them, and the moun-tains seemed no nearer. This was a world without displacement plates ... people walked everywhere.

"Where is the lander?" Sajit said. "I can't see it, it's too dark."

"It's gone!"

The grass was flattened for about twenty meters square. Moonlight silvered the grass-strands. "This world doesn't have any transportation system," said Sajit. "You'll have to go back to the village—"

Elloran had begun walking in the direction of the mountains. The grass seemed to swallow him up. Amid the tall blackness the shimmercloak rippled. "Come back!" Sajit screamed. "You're crazy!"

The boy walked on quickly, not looking back. His eyes were fixed on the mountains. If he wanted to find the Rainbow King it would have to be on foot, all the way. "I won't go," Sajit was yelling into the air. "My foot hurts and you don't know what you're getting into. I don't believe in your philosophies, I just want to eat and sleep!"

He limped after Elloran. The path was just wide enough for a boy to wedge himself through soft grass-stalks. "I don't care about your mission, I just care about *me!* There must be someplace here that isn't full of—" he remembered the room in the moonlight with the unmoving, deathlike family.

Elloran stopped in the distance. "You're right. It's my mission, not yours." He turned his back to Sajit and went on walking.

"Wait!" Sajit thrust hard against the ground, ignoring the limp. Pain lanced his foot as he caught up with Elloran. "I've got all the food."

"Come on."

They went on walking for an eternity. Every step stabbed his foot; he was dizzy from sleeplessness. He heard Elloran muttering, "There must be a displacement plate somewhere. This is supposed to have been one of the most industrialized planets in this area, they must have been industrialized enough to blow up Ainverell...."

"And someone must have disposed of the lander, somehow," said Sajit, out of breath. "It's incomprehensible."

Ahead were the mountains with the rainbows drained of color. They trudged on. Sajit was so tired. Elloran never slacked. *Why am I following him?* Sajit thought. *Just because he wears a shimmercloak? Just through force of habit?* Ahead of him, only the shimmercloak shone, the pink blushing against the dark blue, strangely gaudy in the darkness. The stars of the Dispersal shone on them; the sky was star-thick, except for where the ghosts of rainbows made arches of mist. *We'll never make it anywhere,* Sajit thought. He wondered what death would feel like.

After a while—a couple of klomets, it felt like—the pain in his foot was continual. The grass had thinned and the ground was stubbed with sharp stones. Sajit stumbled, whispered, "Powers of powers! I can't go on. Just leave me here—tomorrow I'll be well enough to forage for myself...."

Elloran looked at him, expressionless. "No. We'll rest."

"What about your infernal mission?"

"The Inquest is compassionate."

"I hope the Inquest bums!" he shouted, unable to control himself.

"Can't you act like a human being instead of a servocorpse?"

"The Inquest is compassionate ... and I do not want to go on alone," Elloran said, looking away. Sajit felt the boy's loneliness and was moved.

They stumbled on for a few more meters. The ground became very smooth—they could not really see what the terrain was—and when they sat down it contoured itself to their bodies. They must be in the foundations of an old house, long since swept away in whatever metamorphosis it was that had changed Ymvyrsh from a wartorn world to an illusion of paradise. The moon had set, and they could hardly see their goal ahead of them but for the jagged eclipsing of the starfield, the serrated black horizon.

"Do you want some food?" Sajit was emptying the bundle.

... jangle of wirestrings, whisper of shadow spirits ...

"You still have that thing?" Elloran said, reaching for one of the packets.

Sajit picked it up. His fingers felt cold immediately. Instinctively he clutched the whisperlyre to his thin chest; he felt the warmth drain from his body. He plucked a few notes, touched the tuning studs to find the pelog mode of the ancients ... the jangle resolved into rainbow resonance misted with sighs....

A song surfaced, fully crystallized—the first song he had ever learnt from the *dorezda* who had taken him off planet and then dumped him on Ont like an old whisperlyre that has lost all its music....

eih! asheveraín amplanzhet ka dhand-eruden,
eih! eskrendaí: pu eyáh chitarans hyemadh?

ai! when man dispersed we wept for the dead earth;
ai, we cried: where is the homeworld of the heart?

At first he was thinking as he sang, I shouldn't do this in

front of an Inquestor who has probably heard all the best singers in the Dispersal, who don't run out of breath in the wrong places, and he didn't pay much attention, so his voice cracked easily. It was a breathy, impure, poignant voice with little conscious artistry. After a while he was able to ignore his companion and to sing only for himself —not the way he used to sing, eyeing the purses of passing strangers—and it was beautiful in the alien night, and full of pain.

Elloran was saying, "You could be good, if you were trained. Didn't the In- questors see to it?"

"I ran away," Sajit said testily. He was surprised that Elloran had been listening to him. Elloran looked away, avoiding conflict. The semi- sentient shimmercloak shone in the pastels that even Sajit knew meant safety, pure air, healthful environment. The song had frozen Sajit's chest, and the breeze made him shiver. Elloran said,

"Yes—the homeworld of the heart. That's what this planet feels like, you know.

My shimmercloak feels it. The meadows. The moun- tains."

"Just words, Inquestor." He had never met anyone who really thought about the words of songs....

"It's a cruel, grotesque parody of a utopia," he heard Elloran say. "It could be a test. Maybe two Grand Inquestors are playing ma- krúgh and they have a wager on me." Sajit didn't really listen; Elloran often talked about things he couldn't visualize ... Grand Inquestors. Or Uran s'Varek, a planet full of Inquestors. Louder, Elloran said, "Do you think we'll ever find it?"

"What?" Sajit's eyelids were heavy and he didn't feel like talking.

"The 'homeworld of the heart', chítarans hyemadh in the high-tongue."

"Who's looking?" mur- mured Sajit through his tiredness. "A twenty-thous- and-year-old song that beg- gar boys sing ..."

"Look at the trouble they've gone to, to create this place!" Elloran's voice was intense. "And I have to

destroy it. Without vin-
dictiveness. Only with compassion. If you were an Inquestor you would under-
stand these things, soldier
boy."

"Don't brood," Sajit
snapped. More kindly, he
said, "Go to sleep."

He let the whisperlyre
slip from his arms and the
warmth ooze back into them.
The breeze played over him. *I
scolded an Inquestor!* he
thought suddenly. But he
wasn't alarmed. He felt
almost happy.

Perhaps it was the cer-
tainty of hopelessness. The
soft wind played like an
afterwhisper, resolving the
dissonance of the day's
terror.

They each took up a
comer of the floor space, as
far as possible from one
another, each treasuring his
aloneness.

***

In the morning, under a
dazzling sun, they scratched
at the earth a meter or two
from the roofless floor, and
they found a displacement
plate.

Sun-drenched, the sky
glowed celadon-blue over the
plate; Elloran stood where
they imagined its center to
be, eyes closed. It was hard to
make out the patches of
mirror metal under the o-
vergrowth of moss and
bramble. Before them, the
mountains and their rainbow
archways, unchanged from
the previous day. Elloran was
subvocalizing commands to
the displacement field
mechanism; Sajit hoped that
it still worked. He moved up
to stand beside the young
Inquestor, bundle slung over
his shoulder. Without
warning, an odd dislocation
—

They were still in the
same place! But no ... weren't
the mountains a little nearer?
He tried to move but found
that his feet were tangled in
brambles. They'd moved
forward perhaps a couple of
klomets, and the landscape
was almost the same, and
everything that had grown
over the displacement plate
had been flicked in with
them.

"Progress!" said Elloran.
But he was disappointed

when he saw how much further the mountains were. "Let's go on walking. We'll he able to uncover another plate soon if we follow the standard patterns...."

They walked for another four hours or so before they uncovered the next one. It was not a standard system, or else some of the plates had been destroyed by time or design. They stopped for a meal—that was the end of the food—and flicked on to the next plate.

Two days went by. The mountains did seem a little nearer. Hunger gnawed at Sajit, but he did not see the Inquestor tire at all. They slept, or tried to, by night; hunger kept Sajit awake. 'There was water sometimes, from a stream; but they seemed to have passed the agricultural lands now, and there were no wild animals they could have trapped and eaten even if either of them had known how.

Why am I going along with him? Sajit kept asking himself. He found no satisfactory answer; and the pain in his stomach blotted out everything, so he stopped asking. Around them, the countryside was beautiful as ever. And ahead—

The rainbows hung, hugging the black mountains, taunting them. Sometimes Sajit would sing, but it made him too cold, and he would stop in midphrase. And Ton Elloran never looked back. An Inquestor was not like a normal person, Sajit thought; even the young ones were different.

On the third day, they found a plate that was scrubbed clean, a silver island in the green sea. When Elloran leapt on to it he cried, "It clicks well, it understands all the subvocalizations!" Sajit saw that he was smiling, a wan little smile, and then Elloran called out in a big voice, "Rainbow King, your reign is ending! 'The Inquest has come!" and they flicked out and—

"They were standing on a ledge, overlooking a tapestry of green fur quilted with fields and embroidered with wavy rivers, and the wind on their faces was cold, and underneath his tiredness even Sajit felt an exaltation creep up.... "These paths are constantly used," he said. "There is someone in the mountains, someone at the end of the rainbows...." They scrambled for the next plate, only ten meters away against a bare wall of fine-grained schist, and then burst up into a higher level. There was a rainbow directly overhead, a cartwheel of colors fused into the intense blue sky. He gave a wild yodel of joy, the mountains echoed like a well-tuned whisperlyre, and then they crossed the brief plateau and gazed over an abrupt chasm that cradled an emerald serpent of a valley, raced to the next plate and were over the chasm on a ledge with a sheer rockface ahead—

"There are no more plates," said Sajit. He felt dismay as though awakened from a dream of soaring.

Elloran vanished behind an outcropping; he had gone to find a displacement plate. "It can't just end like this!" Sajit heard him murmur, and then he turned around, his back to the tall wall that blocked their path, and saw —

A swoop of shadow. A momentary eclipse of the sun ... then a flurry of pink ringed with sunlight, diving, piercing the rainbow....

A pteratyger! he thought. His heart leapt at the sight. It swerved out of the firehalo of sunlight, pink feathered wings outstretched, motionless. The fierce feline features were frozen, inconstruable.

And then, darting from behind the first one like silverdoves, only impossibly far away, a whole exaltation of them, circling, spiralling behind the leader like links in a gene-strand—

"Elloran, come quickly, there are pteratygers!" Sajit shouted. He turned for a moment and ran toward the boulder where he thought his companion had gone. He stood there, out of breath with joy, and then Elloran was pointing, wild with fear, "Sajit, quickly!"

He whirled round. They were wheeling ahead, near enough to see the glow of ember eyes. And then one broke loose and plummeted towards Sajit, wings erect, claws glistening.

It was so beautiful! He froze for a moment, then the soldier in him thrust loose and he dilated his eyes and glared the laser-glare and subvocalized the secret command and—

(Burst of flame, pink feathers drifting, sunlight....)

—the circle shivered, abruptly reformed as a V-line of angry pteratygers arrowed at his face—

And then stopped again. Reformed in no discernible pattern, Sajit saw, they were looking past him now, as though someone had given a command.

He stole a glance behind. Elloran had emerged completely from behind the rocks. His shimmercloak flapped in the wind. For the first time that day Sajit was sick with hunger.

Elloran said, his voice a whisper in the wind, "You dare to assault me, pteratygers, creatures of the Inquest?"

The pteratygers circled uncertainly; a few broke from the flock and swerved up into the wind, rainbowing over the rainbow. Sajit stared at this boy who did not know the simplest thing about self-preservation and yet could face a pteratyger and say simply how dare you. Then one of the creatures swooped swiftly on to the rock-ledge, facing them. Sajit stepped back involuntarily.

"My—lord—" said the pteratyger. A plaintive, screech-edged voice like a songpipe with a broken reed.

"You are far from Uran s'Varek now," Elloran said. "You serve the Rainbow King?"

"Yes—" The cry pierced the wind and Sajit retreated again.

"Why did you attack us?" asked Elloran.

"The soulless one—he should not have penetrated —beyond the rainbow barriers—the King's domain— must be rendered inoperative—"

"Don't harm him!" Elloran hissed. Sajit flinched.

"I do not understand—you are not the King—yet wear the shimmercloak—I am a mere animal—I obey you—"

"Where is the King?"

"In Irísbarah—the rainbow castle—"

"There are no more displacement plates," said Elloran.

"What's a soulless one?" Sajit blurted out, sick with fear.

"I don't know!" Elloran whispered. Sajit froze. Then Elloran said, "Take me to the Rainbow King!" He spoke firmly but his voice cracked on the last word. The pteratyger did not notice the Inquestor's uncertainty. Sajit stared at its face. The teeth glistened like icicles. Then Elloran said, "No. Take me to —where the soulless ones are rendered inoperative...."

"Powers of powers, Elloran, are you trying to kill me?"

"Be quiet!" Sajit was cowed into silence now, the reflex of obedience to the Inquestral word taking over. Even now when they had been through so much. To the pteratyger Elloran said, "I will take the soulless one with me."

"As—you—command—" And then it roared, a thunder with a tinge of miaow in it, and came nearer, and crouched down. Elloran mounted without a word, and beckoned for Sajit to get on behind. Sajit took a few steps and caught the creature's foul breath. He could guess what it must feed on. Taking hold of himself, he swung himself over the furry flanks and dug his knees firmly into its body. A heavy purr shook the animal's body. Without warning—

The pteratyger turned to face the sunlight, flapped its wings resoundingly and sprang into the wind—

A moment of burning nausea. And then the pteratyger righted itself and began to climb, hugging the mountainside and slicing through the bittercold air. Sajit's terror turned to exhilaration.

When he looked behind he saw the mountains they had crossed with such struggling, huge crag-topped tombstones bursting from the lush green earth. They sundered a rainbow, sending shivershards of color streaking and swirling. They were only holo-images, then, those rainbows....

"Why does the pteratyger obey you?" Ssgit had to shout to hear himself.

"They were created a thousand years ago by an Inquestor on Uran s'Varek, genetically altered from earth animals. They were to be part of an immense game of *makrúgh*, you know. They are impelled to obey the shimmercloak—they aren't very intelligent animals."

"What's a soulless one?"

No answer. The pteratyger roared again, its cry shattering the wind's whine, and they soared. The ripple of the animal's muscles under him made Sajit tingle.

Suddenly Elloran cried, "Sajit, you must sing for me, you must—" and he gripped his arm so tightly that it hurt. The touch unnerved Sajit. Inquestors did not cling to soldier boys like children in need. *He has needs,* Sajit

thought, and it was not a comfortable thought.

Gently Sajit freed his arm. He shook his bundle, uncovering the whisperlyre, and the fabric swirled away into a speck. Wedging the whisperlyre firmly between them he sang, very softly, the song about the dream of utopia: *"Eih! asheveratn amplamhet ka dhand-eruden...."* He thought: *We're going to get killed now. I'm sure of it.* He threw his heart into the song, and the meaning of the words became vivid for him for the first time ...

"Shénom na chítarans hye-madhá ... we yearn for the heart's homeworld ...u *áthera tinjéh erúdeh* ... where sun touches earth ... *z'irsai yver tembáraxein kreshpáh* ... and rainbows gird the mountains of darkness ... *z'púrreh y'Enguestren tinjéh* ... and the Inquestor touches the beggar child...." The wind gouged the tears from his cheeks.

His arm still burned from Elloran's desperate grip. He understood his companion a little now. For a moment they had touched, like in the song, as though the utopia for which all men yearned had come already ... it had not felt like an Inquestor's hand. Only like another boy's.

If this is a false utopia, he thought fiercely, how could this have come about? And impulsively—with the cold of the whisperlyre gnawing at him like hunger—he reached out to clasp Elloran's hand.

Elloran stared straight ahead, so Sajit couldn't see his face; but for a moment he thought he felt a responding warmth. Maybe not. Maybe it was only the flush of flesh against the cold.

They thrust through the stinging wind, upwards, ripping through moist veils of mist, bursting over a sea of cloud, and then Sajit saw what lay ahead. The source of rainbows, set on an island peak in the sea of mist ...

Irísbarah. The rainbow castle.

Lucent mother-of-pearl pagodas rose like conch-shells wrenched inside out, their spires criss-crossed with arcs of color, crystal-bright against the brilliant blue sky. They soared high against the sun, then dove in a time-frozen glide towards the castle.

"Look!" Elloran pointed to a railinged platform set on top of a high stone column. "It's a receiving station for a tachyon bubble system!"

Sajit could hardly contain himself "Then there's an Inquestor down there! And—you're an Inquestor, and that means you can arrange to have him send us home, alive, with our bellies full! With a tachyon bubble we can be home today!"

... But there's no home for me, he remembered suddenly. Only the war.

Elloran didn't answer. What was wrong with him? Look at all they'd come through! And now they'd found what they wanted, hadn't they?

They circled the castle a few times. He could almost reach out and touch a pagoda. Then they swooped. He closed his eyes and dreamed of the home he'd never had. But Elloran didn't speak, and Sajit saw that he was in the grip of a terrible tension. "What's the matter with you?" he shouted.

"Don't you understand anything?" Elloran screamed in anguish. "Everything has gone wrong! An Inquestor made this world. He made a dead world of utter beauty and he embalmed it so that it would never change. He's a heretic—a false utopian—a madman, and he's down there and he has power to explode a planet to watch the fireworks! An Inquestor gone insane!" He was shaking with rage.

Sajit asked him no more questions. They hovered over a firewall braceleted with menacing, motionless guards, and he heard the relentless clap of the pteratyger's wings and gave up trying to understand.

The pteratyger took them to a ledge under the castle's foundations, artificially smooth. They scrambled down; and when Sajit turned to face the clouds, he saw the pteratyger already diving through a gap in the forest of rainbow arcs, flashing into the sunlight. His eyes smarted.

"Come on!" Elloran said urgently. Sajit turned to see a cavern with an irising gate that had just responded to Elloran's subvocalized command....

The gate clanged shut. Darkness. A pungent, chemical air. Windlessness. Silence.

"Are you there, Elloran?" he whispered.

The light touch of the Inquestor's hand, brushing his shoulder.

Again the feeling of dislocation, of unreality, of being touched by a person of such power....

"Do you see anything?" Elloran said. The voice startled him.

After a while he could make things out. People, hundreds of people. Not breathing. Standing against the walls, shoved into piles, motionless. Elloran moved towards a pile of bodies. He touched one gingerly. Sajit flinched for him.

"They are all dead."

Sajit said nothing; it wasn't sinking in. "Come on." Holding on to each other, they pushed on into the half dark. They found another door.

The light blinded him for a moment.

Then he saw that they were on a railinged balcony that circled a chamber big as a starship, hollowed out of the rock. There were bodies scattered across the mirror metal floor in stacks, like leafheaps in autumn: old men, children, women. Machines on silent hover-casters darted from body to body, sorting, spraying, restacking them in other piles. ...

Across the hall, doll-sized in the distance, more heaps of sprawling bodies, arranged by age, sex, height, physical attributes.

"Let's go down," said Elloran.

They found a stairway spiralling down to the floor. Sajit gazed upward to see the fan-vaulting of stone rainbows that was echoed in the mirror glitter of the floor. Slowly they walked across the room. It must be three hundred meters across. Each step reechoed as in a temple. Now and then a machine would scuttle up to them, react to Elloran's shimmercloak, scurry off.

"Servocorpses," whispered Elloran. "A servocorpse factory."

Sajit had seen them before, these dead men re-animated into grisly servants, usually walking a few steps behind one of the *dorezdas*, one with a taste for the exotic, the expensive ... he already knew what Elloran must be thinking.

"All the people on this planet," he said.

"Yes," said Elloran. "They're all dead."

Another displacement plate—

Valleys of dead bodies, unprocessed, unembalmed, still reeking, suspended in huge storage fields....

Rows of blank-eyed children, their limbs wrenched off by war machines, row after row of old men emaciated by warplagues ...

Cosmetic rooms, skeletons plastifleshed into life ...

A bridge over another chamber where the dead walked round and round in an eerie procession, smiles soldered on their faces ...

More displacement plates ...

They crossed another bridge over a chasm of crematoria, choking with the smoke of incinerating bodies ... they passed dressing rooms where dead bodies stood stiffly to be decked out in new tunics bright with rainbow dyes and where metal arms patted their hair into shape and rouged their cheeks ... the whole mountain was a labyrinth, level upon level, peopled with the dead.

It was the silence that was most appalling. All the machines moved noiselessly. And the people, beautiful in death, did not breathe ... then there were other rooms where autosurgeons were hard at work, clipping cyberinputs into place, and there were rooms where the dead ones walked in circles, their muscles twitching to the movements of unseen strings, and, finally, rooms where the dead ones—row upon row of them—stood talking to the nothingness: Ifs a fine day. The crops are good this season. We welcome you, visitor.

And they found another room where holoimages monitored the ring of clean displacement plates in the foothills. They watched a fresh servocorpse, a young man laughing as the wind made his fresh clothes flap, appear on the plate, run down toward the village, his face flushed with mechanical joy....

"Somewhere in this mountain," said Elloran, "is a machine that runs everything on the planet. A think-hive of such power that only an Inquestor could have requisitioned it ..."

"At night they turn them off," said Sajit, remembering the room of living statues. Not~living statues. "And they don't really eat, but they have food, make-believe food, and make-believe agriculture...."

"The thinkhive is programmed for utopia, is primed with the things men yearn for but cannot have...."

"No wonder the planet seems like old Earth—the lost homeworld of the heart...."

"Myths, myths, Sajit-without-a-clan!" Elloran chided. But without anger. "If old Earth ever was, if the Dispersal of Man ever really took place, do you think it was really a paradise from which we fell?

The breaking of joy is the beginning of wisdom."

They watched the monitor for a few moments. It showed the empty fields, the sky, the sun setting.

"Everybody's dead," Elloran said tonelessly.

It was too big for fear. Sajit could feel nothing at all, not even the ache of emptiness. Even his hunger left him.

"The war's over," Elloran went on, "and now I have to go and deal with whoever it is who has made this...."

He moved towards the displacement plate. Sajit knew he was going to go into the castle. "Don't do it!" he cried out. The sound rebounded like a broken whisperlyre. But he knew it was no use. He clutched his instrument and followed Elloran, hypnotized by the boy's eyes, the weary eyes of an old man.

A courtyard. Guards pacing. Sunset. Ahead, a towering portal flanked with iridescent columns, massive gateways inlaid with mother-of-pearl.

Elloran and Sajit stepped off the displacement plate. Guards wheeled, weapons pointing. They were surrounded.

"Laser them," Elloran hissed.

"But—"

"They're already dead!" Elloran ducked and Sajit opened his eyes wide and whirled, squeezing the power from them with the subvocalized words—

Sizzle, bisected bodies snapping, thudding.

"The castle." Elloran walked to the gates; they dissolved. They stepped into an Inquestral throne room.

It was a giant's domain. Flagstones, fire-etched marble from Ont, each four or five meters square, stretched out like a makrugh board.

Columns topped with fire-fountains ringed them. Their footsteps shifted and echoed like the voices of ghosts....

"Rainhow King!" Elloran shouted. His own voice returned, echo-rich, taunting. Above them a mobile of rainbows twirled slowly, layer upon layer of them crossing the hall's high ceiling, which glowed all over with soft prism-fringed light. "Rainbow King! Come out and meet your Inquestor and Envoy of the High Inquestors, messenger of Uran s'Varek!" Only echoes. It was as if they were inside a gigantic whisperlyre.

At the end of the hall was an empty throne.

"This is it, then," said Sajit. It was hard not to whisper. "This is the end. There's no one here."

"If we go out now and find the tachyon controls still working, I should be able to get us away from here," Elloran said hoarsely. It seemed so unsatisfying, to come here, to reach the lair of the Rainbow King, and to find only an empty castle ... Sajit could not understand his own disappointment. Why should he care? It was not his mission. It was not his quest.

"Let's look around a little more," said Sajit. They approached the foot of the throne, and he pointed to a displacement plate. They looked at each other for a moment. Sajit shrugged listlessly. "Why not?" They flicked out—

Another vast room, a perfect sphere a hundred meters high, walled with thousands upon thousands of interlocking hexagons, like a honeycomb ... each hexagon was a two-dimensional monitor. The surface of the sphere was all gravi-down. Slowly they walked around. In the monitors—

Smiling children. Startling sunsets. Aerial views of villages, pretty patterns of white flecks in the greenery. Laughing old men telling tales around a table. Skies festooned with rainbows. Flocks of silverdoves, star-bright in the clear sky. A million eyes looking out on the planet of the dead.

In the center of the sphere, sitting in a hover-floating throne, was an old man.

Elloran was white.

The hoverthrone drifted toward them. Sajit saw the old man's face, parched and pale under a wisp of white hair. And the eyes ... where had he seen such terrible, haunted eyes before, such weary, sunken, despairing eyes?

"Loreh, Taanyel's son. My old pupil." The old man's voice was barely audible, as if he had not spoken for years. "After all this, they send me you...."

Elloran said, "Ton Alkamathdes, I am Ton Elloran n'Taanyel Tath, Inquestor-who-is-to-be. You have broken the law, Ton Alkamathdes. You've created an illusory utopia. For what, Alkamathdes? You've"—his voice cracked, and Sajit was dismayed for a moment that he might burst into tears —"you've gone against everything that you taught me yourself, Ton Alkamathdes! How could you betray us all like this?"

"Loreh, Loreh"—Sajit saw Elloran flinch at the old man's use of the diminutive —"They were killing each other! There was so much hate here! All I did was wipe out the source of their hate, the other planet ... what was wrong with that? We've destroyed a thousand planets for less ... now they don't hate anymore. Now they love each other, all my children, and they live in paradise."

"You're a heretic—setting yourself up as god—killing without compassion—you're insane!"

"Insane?" Alkamathdes laughed, a dry, rasping sound like leaves in the wind. "I'm perfectly sane. But the Inquest, the Dispersal of Man, the human race—ha! ha!" He raised his hand and the throne came nearer still, hovering only a few meters from the two of them.

"I weep for you," said Elloran. But he did not weep.

Alkamathdes smiled, a twisted smile. "I took their murderous, selfish passions upon myself, Loreh. How can you say I was not compassionate? They did not have to kill anymore. I gave them freedom from their human condition ...." He gestured wildly at the scenes on the monitors. "My eyes, see! I see the joy in the world, and I am content that my children love me." He rose and stood at the foot of his hoverthrone, and Sajit saw that his shimmercloak was tattered and threadbare and had ceased to shine.

"I repeat the formula for your release from the Inquest, Alkamathdes, in the highspeech and the lowspeech," Elloran said steadily. "Listen and understand. *Den eis Enguester! Din rilacho st' Enguestaran! Evendek eká eis! Enguesti tembres! Enguesti dhandas!*" His voice rose. "You are no Inquestor! I release you from the Inquestors! You are alone forever! You are dark to the Inquest! You are dead to the Inquest!" The throne dove towards them like a pteratyger.

"You think you can stop me with words, with official formulas, Loreh? What empty ideas have they been feeding you? Look at me. I'm your teacher, your master. I know what is good for you. I'll send you home. Just keep quiet about this—"

"You had our ship destroyed!"

"Of course, of course, had to protect my children from you utopia destroyers. ..."

"Laser him, Sajit!" The old man had raised up a hand to summon something—

Sajit glared at the old man and tried to subvocalize the word but the shimmercloak rippled through the tatters and he couldn't bring himself to—

"He's calling his dead guards, he's going to kill us!" Elloran screamed. Sajit raised his whisperlyre and threw it with his last strength at the old man's head, thinking I can't be doing this I can't be attacking an Inquestor—

Monitors splintered. Broken whisperstrings jangled. For a second the old man tottered, defying gravity. Then he crumpled from his throne. Sajit looked away.

Before the tears bleared his eyes, he saw in the monitors—

Children toppling in heaps, men and women collapsing in mid-action, machines grinding to a halt, a lone child plummeting from a treetop with a frozen smile—

The monitors went blank. The whole machinery must have been cued to the old man's brain-patterns. He had linked with the thinkhive and now both were dead.

Elloran strode over to the limp form, crouched over the ragged body, and tore the shimmercloak from the body, ripping the fabric with a fierce, childish anger. He was screaming, "You betrayed me, Alkamathdes! I believed everything you taught me and you betrayed me!" He hammered the corpse with his fists again and again, like an automaton, until he was worn out, and Sajit realized slowly that he had killed an Inquestor.

Then Elloran drew himself up tall and straightened his shimmercloak and came to Sajit. He had composed his face now, and Sajit knew that he would never lose control of himself again. It was when he looked in Elloran's eyes that he remembered the eyes of the dead Inquestor. They were the same eyes, eyes of power and of tragedy.

Elloran said, "Now we can go and find the tachyon bubble system."

Sajit went to find his whisperlyre. It was broken beyond repair, so he laid it over the body and drew a fragment of frayed shimmercloak over it. It had been the last link to his childhood. "There'll be others," Elloran said gently. "Now listen."

They faced each other in the huge chamber. A million blank hexagonal eyes stared at them from all sides. Sajit glanced at the body and shied away from it. Elloran said, "Sajit, I have hunted my first utopia. I am no longer an Inquestor-who-is-to-be. I have reached my power now. Do you know what that means, Sajit? Do you know what power means? This shall be my first act—" He held his hand out over Sajit. Instinctively Sajit knelt. "I name you to the clan of Shen, soldier Sajit. You are free from the wars now. I hope you'll be a great musician one day."

Sajit rose. He glowed with quiet elation. He wanted to embrace his companion, to thank him, to share this joy. But he couldn't.

Now they could not be friends. They could not touch. The illusion of utopia was over. The homeworld of the heart was for poets, for dreamers. Not for survivors. Sajit understood this.

So all he said was, "Thank you. Lord Inquestor. It's what I've always wanted." Then, impulsively, he added, "You have so much power, you Inquestors! You can make planets that conform to men's dreams, you can make my dreams come true. If only I were like you—"

In the huge chamber, over the Inquestor's body, they almost touched. Then Elloran said softly, "You don't understand, do you?" He sounded bitter. "It is *I* who wish—"

He stopped himself. Sajit knew that there were things Inquestors may not wish. That was how things were.

After a moment, to break the silence, Elloran said, "Shen Sajit, one day"—he laughed shyly—"I hope you will teach me that song."

"It will have to be soon," Sajit said, "before my voice changes." But he knew they were just acting now, clinging to the last moments of the utopia as the ear clings to a whisperlyre's shimmerfade after the song is done.

DESPATCHES FROM EARTH

The End of Chapter Nine
Reflections on the Year of Mourning for the King of Thailand

by S.P. Somtow

I began writing this note in October 2017, on the last day of the official mourning period. I haven't finished it and now it's only a few hours until 2018. Perhaps it's time ...

The year of official mourning has passed, yet one has yet to see the streets of Bangkok explode into kaleidoscopic color. I put away the black clothes on Sunday and took a long look at the piles of untouched shirts of every hue, and I couldn't bring myself to make a simple decision I haven't made for a year — what to wear? I opted in the end for white ... as it were, a delaying tactic.

There is still a lot of reluctance to let go. This is not surprising; if we were to think of the Chakri Dynasty as an epic novel, then Chapter Nine was the most exciting, the most tumultuous, the most "unputdownable" of all its chapters so far. In the course of Chapter Nine, a quaint, somewhat exotic backwater kingdom that was not really on the world's radar became a significant member of the international community. Its food topped the popularity scale. Its movies won awards. Its martial arts became known as the coolest, most "badass". Its inhabitants moved from a two-tier society of have-nots and have-everythings towards one with an increasingly powerful and vocal middle class. Its capital city became the world's most coveted tourist destination.

This chapter had a dark side, too. True representational democracy had a brief flowering in the 1970s following decades of an authoritarian system, but since then the country has yoyoed back and forth between shades of dictatorship and democracy, each often donning the deceptive plumage of the other. Corruption ran rampant, with the accusers often as corrupt as the accused. The Buddhist principles which are meant to underpin this society, detachment, compassion, and unselfishness, were often riddled with greed and self-advancement.

Yet high above the drama, the trauma, the turbulence, the figure of King Rama IX appeared as an icon of that which is good in us. He was to many a beacon of security, a symbol that some values remain unchanging. He was loved in a way that foreigners found difficult to comprehend. And it was in his person that Thais found a potent symbol for an exceptionalism that became the very essence of the nation's sense of identity.

There have been very few people in history able to sustain the weight of such iconography. That this happened in

Thailand, at just the time that it was needed, was an amazing stroke of national karma. For unlike many of the world's hereditary rulers, King Rama IX was not "born to be king." Political squabbles and a devastating family tragedy were what thrust him into this position.

That this jazz-playing, fast-car-driving young man, raised in Europe, this sophisticated polyglot, this man of the world, had the courage to take upon himself this burden; that he was able to find within himself a voice of strength and calm that could bring a sense of stability to the country even in the most turbulent of times; that he had the vision to steer a mediaeval kingdom into a chaotic future with a sense of its integrity, independence, and uniqueness; this was a one-of-a-kind feat. His achievements were monumental.

But monumental achievements alone could not have engendered this outpouring of love from Thailand's millions. There was something more. Naturally, people loved and respected the institution; that is something inculcated in every iteration of values, taught in schools and reinforced by media, a reflection of the pyramidal structure of this society. But this love paled in comparison to the love people felt for the person himself.

This love came from the knowledge that King Bhumibol never forgot the lessons of his childhood, living in a "normal" people's world, raised by a singularly brave and resourceful single mother. No matter how high he was elevated, ordinary people still felt that he understood their world, their concerns. When you look beyond the extravagant encomiums, you get to a core of true feeling.

I remember, as most Thais do I am sure, the exact moment that I learned that the Chapter Nine had ended. I was about to conduct a big concert at an event to which dozens of important politicians of Asia had been invited, hosted by the Ministry of Foreign Affairs, at the luxurious Plaza Athenée Hotel. We had just had a an extraordinarily brilliant rehearsal, and it was as I was leaving the hall that one of the Directors General whispered to me, "It's happened."

It fell to me to tell the musicians, who were waiting to perform, having their boxed lunches in a suite nearby. As I walked into the room, I simply said, "I don't think I have to tell you why tonight's concert has been cancelled." A curtain of grief fell on the room. The old cliché, "palpable silence", was real. It was the silence of an entire country.

The Chapter had ended, but it would take a year to turn the page.

The year began with an immense outpouring of grief that welled up from everywhere. Because of an unexpected phone call from HSH Prince Mui, the well known film director, I ended up having three days to organize the a performance of the Royal Anthem in front of the Grand Palace, an even in which (according to some, but who was counting) up to 300,000 people participated. The astounding thing about this event was how unplanned it really was. We had estimated a chorus of a hundred, an orchestra of a hundred to lead the singing, but by the time we were setting up there were over two hundred in the orchestra and many more in the choir, including singers from other countries, a direct descendant of His Majesty, children from the Klong Toei slum area, and members of several Bangkok-based choirs. There are several videos of this event including the one that the prince himself filmed, shown in movie theaters for many months, but nothing can convey what it was really like.

In spite of the country's traumatic divisions, there was a oneness that day, and it was a oneness made possible by the sheer personal charisma of our departed King.

During the year, things were muted. We all did different things to help hold on to the legacy. I organized a huge, packed concert of the complete works of the King, played by all the best orchestras, jazz ensembles, singers, choirs, and soloists I could coral. I realized that although King

Bhumibol's tunes are widely disseminated, and have played in shopping malls and on TV and in hundreds of different arrangements, there are still some melodies that were relatively unknown. Seeing the entire oeuvre in a single day, from waltzes to marches, from romantic ballads to quirky blues numbers, was a revelation for many about the sheer eclecticism of his musical taste. I hope this will become an annual event; we plan another such in 2018.

The year ended with a an event exponentially huger than our spontaneous outpouring in the days after the King's passing. This was the Royal Cremation: a whole year in the planning, involving artisans, musicians, pageantry, and focusing the attention of the world on the monumental but temporary structures created for the ancient rituals. It was solemn. It was sacerdotal. It was spectacular. It was

sweeping. It was an international media sensation.

This was an event as different as possible from what transpired the year before. It was planned down to the second. Nothing was left to chance. There was no chaos. It was a different kind of beauty: stately, dignified, befitting Thailand's sense of nationhood.

The contrast between the two "vast" events which bookended this year of mourning is an instructive one, because when taken together, they are a sort of yin-yang snapshot of Thailand's identity — or at least the perception of that identity.

A day before the cremation, I was walking outside one of the gargantuan malls near my house. A huge open air screen had been set up for people to watch the preparations. As I entered the courtyard, I heard a Thai *piphat* ensemble strike up the Royal Anthem. From a different direction, a military band played the same melody. The two performances, jarringly, were in different keys at the same time. Each played all the way to the end, a little out of sync, and strikingly off key relative to each other, while perfectly consistent with itself.

I had a sort of mild epiphany then, because I understood that to the Thai way of thinking, these performances did not conflict with each other, but were disparate elements in a sort of meta-performance; that what some western critics view as stridently hypocritical is a willingness to accept the validity of conflicting viewpoints, each in its own context. The great American musician who became more Thai than me, Bruce Gaston, once told me that the *ngaan wat* or temple fair is the essence of Thai creativity ... an exuberant concord imposed over chaos. It has taken me a long time to understand this.

It goes back to Buddhist principles, in which we hold that *all* is illusion.

The genius of the Thai sensibility is its ability to hold different, even contradictory visions of reality in a kind of equilibrium, and to create a new structure out of the tensions between them. This sometimes causes us to be viewed as hypocrites, or as a nation that "bends like reed in the wind." But then again, Thailand's national poet, Sunthorn Phu, once said:

> The mighty god Brahma
> has but four faces:
> the citizens of Siam
> have many, many more.

As we headed toward the chapter break, we were worried about many things. Would the present impasse in our country become frozen in place as people are lulled into apathy, or are we heading towards a furious and wrenching collision? But for many of us, our worries about the fate of Thailand were overshadowed by world events. If a country as mighty as the United States can be taken over by a narcissistic madman who could wreck the world's environment or plunge it into nuclear war, what hope does Thailand have? Plenty, I believe. As long as we took the year-long stasis to listen to each other.

Today it is finally 2018. I woke up this morning and didn't want to face a whole new year — and went straight back to bed. I woke up again at 4 pm. As the sun sets on day one of the new chapter, I think I see hope ahead. As long as it has not yet happened, *anything* can happen.

I suspect that what happens next will not be anything anyone ever predicted. Pandora's box keeps yawning wider, but Hope is still with us. So, finally, let's turn the page.

Notes from Beyond the Overcosm
an essay about the Inquestor Series

by Johne Cook

Erasmus wrote "In the land of the blind, the one-eyed man is king." That adage occurs to me whenever I think about Somtow Sucharitkul, one of the most amazing authors of the 80s, a man whose fiction exploded onto the scene in the early 80s and then who, after a strong run into the 90s, for all intents and purposes, disappeared. His works were all over bookstore shelves when I haunted them but you'd be hard pressed to find them now if you didn't know to look for them. This is madness. I have been hoping for decades to see more stories in the Inquestor universe.

Before the internet, if you were a fan of Science Fiction and Fantasy, you found things to read in one of two places - magazines or print novels. I was introduced to The Inquestor series with the novella *Light on the Sound* in the August 1980 issue of Isaac Asimov's Science Fiction Magazine before it was rebranded simply as Asimov's sometime later. The story featured a teenage girl gifted with sight in a community of the blind, only her sight threatened to brand her a pariah, someone who didn't fit in with the rest of her culture. She met a teenage boy who questioned why his people grew and shipped food for others, but for whom and to where? The boy was destined for a life so grand and so terrible that it threatened to overwhelm his sense of right and wrong.

I was already a fan of lyrical Science Fiction thanks to Roger Zelazny, himself a master of poetic, mind-expanding Speculative Fiction. The pullquote which has stuck with me all these years is this one from The Washington Post: "Somtow can create a world with less apparent effort than some writers devote to creating as small room." This was apparent to me in the early 80s as I watched Somtow's fiction explode on the scene.

James Davis Nicoll wrote "Somtow's four book Inquestor series (novels *Light on the Sound, Throne of Madness, The Darkling Wind* and the collection *Utopia Hunters)* is a bleak examination of a galaxy dominated by an autocracy whose claims to compassion fail to conceal that they utterly lack such a quality." Given the current political climate during the mid-point of President Trump's first four year term, the series was practically prophetic.

It's a little ironic that the Inquestors who destroyed utopias had created their own debased version of perfection which benefited only the most powerful, and that the only way to save true utopia was to destroy the false one bent on the destruction of any hint of perfection. It is not the first time we've seen something wicked grow out of noble intent.

The concepts in the Inquestor books were dizzying - traveling the expanse of the entire universe in the blink of an eye using tachyon bubbles, playing games of chance where the cost of losing was the destruction of an entire planet, proclaiming compassion while finding and destroying utopias because Mankind is fallen and must be delivered 'from the throes of delusion.' This was heady stuff.

I instantly fell in love with the expanse of the tale, the lyrical storytelling, the mind-blowing concepts. I loved the story before I learned that this series fit in a genre called 'Space Opera.' I later expanded my love of Space Opera as founder and editor of Ray Gun Revival magazine, a publication which ran from 2006 to 2012 online. I ran into Somtow on Facebook in 2007 and we chatted at that time about an Inquestor revival of some form or another. It is now 2018 and this revival is finally coming to fruition.

All I know is this - an Inquestor does not weep but when I found there would be new Inquestor stories, I did, just a little.

The Inquestor Series

The Novels

Light on the Sound (1982)
The Throne of Madness (1983)
Utopia Hunters (1984)
The Darkling Wind   (1985)

Homeworld of the Heart (in process)
    Part One: *The Singing Moons* (2018)
    Part Two: *A Woman Cloaked in Shadows*
            (coming soon)
    more parts to be announced

in process
Vara's World

The Short Stories

The Thirteenth Utopia (Analog, 1979)
The Web Dancer (IASFM, 1979)
Darktouch (IASFM, 1980) (non-canonical)
Light on the Sound (IASFM, 1980)
The Rainbow King (IASFM, 1981)
The Dust (IASFM, 1981)
Remembrances (IASFM, 1982)
Scarlet Snow (IASFM, 1982)
The Comet that Cried for its Mother (Amazing, 1984)

www.ingramcontent.com/pod-product-compliance
Lightning Source LLC
Chambersburg PA
CBHW030622130626
46552CB00002B/680